Samuel French Acting Edition

Perfect Crime

by Warren Manzi

SAMUELFRENCH.COM   SAMUELFRENCH.CO.UK

FOR PRODUCTION ENQUIRIES

UNITED STATES AND CANADA
Info@SamuelFrench.com
1-866-598-8449

UNITED KINGDOM AND EUROPE
Plays@SamuelFrench.co.uk
020-7255-4302

Each title is subject to availability from Samuel French, depending upon
country of performance. Please be aware that *PERFECT CRIME* may
not be licensed by Samuel French in your territory. Professional and
amateur producers should contact the nearest Samuel French office or
licensing partner to verify availability.

MUSIC USE NOTE

Licensees are solely responsible for obtaining formal written permission from copyright owners to use copyrighted music in the performance of this play and are strongly cautioned to do so. If no such permission is obtained by the licensee, then the licensee must use only original music that the licensee owns and controls. Licensees are solely responsible and liable for all music clearances and shall indemnify the copyright owners of the play(s) and their licensing agent, Samuel French, against any costs, expenses, losses and liabilities arising from the use of music by licensees. Please contact the appropriate music licensing authority in your territory for the rights to any incidental music.

IMPORTANT BILLING AND CREDIT REQUIREMENTS

If you have obtained performance rights to this title, please refer to your licensing agreement for important billing and credit requirements.

Perfect Crime　opened on April 17, 1987 at The Courtyard Playhouse, in New York City. It was directed by Jeffrey Hyatt. The scenic design was by Chris Pickart, the costumes by Barbara Blackwood, the lighting by John Sellars, and the sound by Phil Lee and Tim Pritchard. Graphics by Jay Stone. The production stage manager was Tim Pritchard, and the cast was as follows:

MARGARET THORNE BRENT............Catherine Russell
INSPECTOR JAMES ASCHER.............. Perry Pirkkanen
W. HARRISON BRENT .... G Gordon Cronce
LIONEL MCAULEY .... Marc Lutsky
DAVID BREUER .... W. MacGregor King

The play was first produced by The Actors Collective, and then joined by The Methuen Company, Armand Hyatt, Executive Producer.

Perfect Crime underwent major changes while running, and switched locations Off-Broadway four more times: The Second Stage, The Forty-Seventh Street Theatre, Intar, The Harold Clurman Theatre, and then Theater Four where it was still running as of January 1, 1993. The lighting was by Ann Marie Brady, the sound by David Lawson, and the production stage manager was Carol Dawes. The cast was as follows:

MARGARET THORNE BRENT............Catherine Russell
INSPECTOR JAMES ASCHER................ Warren Manzi
W. HARRISON BRENT .... Mark Johannes
LIONEL MCAULEY .... J.A. Nelson
DAVID BREUER .... Dean Gardner

ACKNOWLEDGEMENTS

There are six people who are personally responsible for the success of this play. Way back, when the script was too long, and too many people were confused, these six had the trust, the belief, and the guts to endure the longest set of previews in the history of the American theatre. The play opened on April 17, 1987, but it wasn't until the summer of 1989 that the last piece of the puzzle fell into place. Imagine how lonely these six felt during that time. They are: Catherine Russell, Armand Hyatt, Jay Stone, Victor Ouimet, Susan Dimond, and Brian Dowd. Thank you so much.

I would also like to thank the actors, designers, technicians, theatre managers, and administrators who have contributed greatly to the process of *Perfect Crime* as it has developed through its Off-Broadway run. Without their expertise and infinite patience, all would have been lost. They are: Evan Georges, Rob Graham, Frank Maraden, Michael Wilding, John Rensenhouse, Michael Worth, James Farrell, Max Storch, John Wojda, Lee Blatteau, Marc Prinz, George Elmer, Tom Morrisey, Craig Mathers, Rosa Vega, Jane MacPherson, Jerry Isaacs, and Larry Staroff.

W.M.

"There's no such thing as the perfect crime."

Unknown

CHARACTERS

MARGARET THORNE BRENT, Psychiatrist. Thirties.

INSPECTOR JAMES ASCHER, The Law. Late thirties.

W. HARRISON BRENT, Margaret's husband. Also a psychiatrist. Forties. Retired.

LIONEL MCAULEY, A patient of Margaret's. Late thirties.

DAVID BREUER, Host of a local cable television show. Thirties.

TIME

Present day.

SCENE

The action takes place in and around the sitting room of the Brent home in Windsor Locks, Connecticut, an out-of-the-way, wealthy community.

This is the kind of community where you might find an Ivan Lendl, or a David Letterman. There's privacy, full privacy, and a healthy arrangement with the Chamber of Commerce.

The house would strongly reflect Margaret's personality.

There cannot be any windows on the set. There's a skylight. With hanging plants.

I believe the style of the sitting room should key off of wood. Very solid. There are bookcases with books. On one shelf is a trophy.

The symmetry of the room will change with every production; however, there are character traits about the sitting room that should be built in. And the text that follows assumes these same character traits. When I refer to Margaret's office, for example, I will assume that the reader knows, or has come to know, that the office and the staircase are on the same side of the room, and therefore on the opposite side of the entrance to the kitchen and the ornate fireplace-front.

That would put the door leading outside on the horizontal wall.

The staircase could be a full one, or just a few steps to a landing. Some form of elevation (top of stairs or landing) is required.

Margaret uses the office and the sitting room for consultations.

There should be some comfortable furniture in the room. And a coffee table that holds magazines and a tray with pastry. It should become apparent that the use of practical lighting on the set is mandatory.

The kitchen leads to a back door (unseen), and a cellar door (also unseen).

The entrance to the kitchen should be angled away from the audience.

The fireplace-front has a surrealistic-type painting painted on the brick. (The description of the painting will appear in the text.)

There is no television set in the sitting room. In Scene 2, Margaret will have rolled out a T.V. set from the kitchen. It should have a VCR unit sitting on top of it.

Also in the room should be a stereo system and a telephone. The phone should sit on a masculine-looking desk and a chair.

I think this desk and stereo should be near one another, and on the same side of the room as the staircase (and, of course, Margaret's office door.)

ACT I

Scene 1	Sunday Night	Ten o'clock
Scene 2	Monday Night	Seven thirty
Scene 3	Tuesday Afternoon	Two-ten
Scene 4	Wednesday Night	Eight o'clock

INTERMISSION

ACT II

Scene 5	Friday Night	Nine o'clock
Scene 6	Saturday Afternoon	Two-twenty
Scene 7	Sunday Night	Ten o'clock

ACT I

Scene 1

*Sunday Night. Ten o'clock. From the darkness
we hear a CLOCK chime ten times. As the
room becomes visible we see only three
sources of light, each so isolated as to create a
dimly-lit, mysterious-looking sitting room.*

*The three sources are MOONLIGHT, one small
NIGHT LIGHT at the top of the stairs, and the
stand-up READING LAMP behind the
armchair.*

The door to the kitchen is closed.

*A MAN enters the room from the front door. HE is
wearing a tuxedo and is bone dry. HE checks
his watch. Suddenly the STEREO goes on,
perhaps operated by a timer. As though taking
a cue, HE moves swiftly to a desk, opens a
drawer and takes out a .45 automatic.
Military issue. Closes drawer. Examines
weapon. Looks around. Opens office door.
Turn on OFFICE LIGHT.*

*The PHONE rings. The MAN turns the MUSIC
down – quickly snatches up the receiver. The
kitchen door will open slowly; a hand will
appear, clutching the door. The man won't see
this.*

11

MAN. (*On phone.*) Yes. (*Short pause.*) HELLO? (*Short pause.*) WE HAVE A BAD CONNECTION – YOU'LL HAVE TO TALK LOUDER; THERE'S A THUNDERSTORM – MARGARET? IS THAT YOU? YOU'RE MUCH TOO LATE; I'VE ALREADY STARTED – I'M DRIPPING WET FROM THE STORM; I COULDN'T FIND THE JOLLY OLD OUTSIDE LIGHT SWITCH SO I GOT A BRANCH AND KNOCKED IT OUT – IT'S MARVELOUS OUTSIDE; CAN YOU HEAR ME? WHAT? DID I TAKE MY INSULIN SHOT? – NO – HA HA HA – I DON'T NEED THEM ANYMORE! – THE PLAY HAS STARTED, puppy – we're in the middle of it now – the clock has chimed; the music is playing. YOU WERE TOO BUSY giving your speech when I called – How *are* your British Club friends? Did they give you the trophy? Did you describe the "perfect crime?" You know I've *seized* on your plan; you'll publish the book, divorce me and live forever with Phillip Reynolds – yes? Pardon my giddiness, but we only have SECONDS left – I'm using your timers, you see; I've got it ALL WORKED OUT FINALLY – YOU'VE ALWAYS BELIEVED I WAS USING MY ILLNESS AS AN EXCUSE FOR FAILURE, BUT YOU COULDN'T SEE THAT YOU WERE HOLDING ME BACK, MARGARET; I WOULD'VE BEEN GREAT! I COULD'VE OVERCOME ANYTHING IF YOU HAD REALLY LOVED ME, IF–

GIRL'S VOICE. (*Offstage, upstairs.*) HARRY!

MAN. (*Yelling upstairs.*) NO, YOU DON'T COME DOWN YET! NOT UNTIL THE WOMAN SAYS "I HATE YOU!" – WE'RE NOT THERE YET! (*Back into phone.*) HELLO? WHAT? (*Slight pause.*) Didn't you recognize the voice, Margaret? I've got your patient here – Carlotta Donovan's upstairs in a green dress; can you guess what we're doing? DO YOU SEE MY PLAN NOW? *STOP TALKING!* Don't you know what the newspapers will say tomorrow?

(*Another TIMER in the office goes off. We will hear a thunderstorm, and then a girl's voice. On tape.*)

MAN. (*To phone.*) There's your other timer, Margaret – we're getting to the woman's voice from your office. What? (*Short pause.*) DON'T TELL ME YOU LOVE ME – YOU'RE JUST TRYING TO SAVE YOURSELF – IT'S ALL OVER – GOODBYE, MARGARET! (*Hangs up quickly.*)

(*The MAN sits in the armchair. HE starts to pick up a magazine, but quickly grabs a piece of cake first, spills some crumbs, curses, snatches up the magazine. Eats. THUNDER.*)

VOICE. (*From office.*) Dr. Brent, Margaret, I'm using your tape recorder. I know you're at the British Club. I was listening on the phone. I yelled out "Harry" on purpose. I wanted you to come back. I wanted you to find us. You caused this; don't you see how you've caused this? You're just getting ready to leave again. You never wanted me to tell you the truth. I hate you. Well, I've killed him. Finally. So my nightmare has come true, yours is just beginning.

(*A GIRL in a green dress appears on the landing. SHE has blazing red hair. We can't see her face. The MAN stands up and points his gun at her. SHE produces a gun and FIRES. The MAN collapses to the floor, dropping the gun, and begins to crawl towards the office. The GIRL keeps FIRING. The MAN disappears into the office. The GIRL follows, stands in the doorway, then goes in, shutting the door behind her. The hand clutching the kitchen door disappears.*)

VOICE. (*From
office contd.*)
But don't worry,
Margaret, I know
there's no such
thing as the perfect
crime. So I've left
you one clue .
(*Slight pause.*)
Goodbye.
(*Thunder.*)   **BLACKOUT**

Scene 2

Monday Night. Seven thirty.
From the blackout we hear sound coming from a
    television set. MUSIC. VOICES. The
    following will be heard in the blackout.

ON TV. (*Voice
of David Breuer.*)
IT'S MONDAY
NIGHT!

MY GUEST IS
MARGARET
THORNE BRENT!

LIVE ACTION.

(*The stage LIGHTS
start coming up.
The sitting room of
the Brent Home.
The next night.
Seven thirty P.M.
The office door is
open. Someone is in
there. Sounds of
DRILLING. Wood.
A T.V. set has been
rolled on, with a
VCR Unit sitting on
it.The VCR
LIGHTS are on.
The T.V. Screen is
visible to the
audience.*

ON TV. (*Voice of David Breuer.*) DO THE CLOSE-UP, LESLIE!

LIVE ACTION. (*PHONE rings. Enter MARGARET THORNE BRENT. From her office. Walking deliberately towards the T.V. set. SHE's carrying an electric drill with screw bit. SHE is wearing a kind of painter's smock. The smock is covered in paint. Mostly red. SHE stands menacingly in front of the T.V. set. SHE puts drill down on armchair.*)

ON TV.
(*We see DAVID
BREUER. Thirties.
HE's mellow.
DAVID will talk to
us.*)

LIVE ACTION.
(*PHONE rings.
PHONE rings
again.
MARGARET
answers phone.*)

MARGARET.
Hello. Who is this?
I'VE TOLD YOU;
MY HUSBAND IS
NOT HERE
RIGHT NOW!
(*Slight pause.*) Oh,
Brenner's
Pharmacy. What
do YOU want? No, I
always keep extra
insulin for him.
I'm a doctor,
remember? Yes, I
know where your
pharmacy is

DAVID.
(*Not all this dialogue will be audible. See stage directions in other column.*) Hey, dudes! Welcome to my show! (*CU of David.*) It's local cable like it MUST BE! Yeah! I'm feeling good today. I had a good night last night. Yeah! I know most of you are at Paul and Bobby's Sunset Lounge on Route Eleven. I'm there, too! Yeah! Cause I taped my show this morning. HEY! HI, ME!! But, hey, last night I got blasted! I mean, like wasted! But, listen: I gotta do the rapping part of my program. Okay. So here's my guest. She's a doctor.

located. (*SHE clicks the phone.*) Hello? Oh hi! Yah, I'm watching it now. He's an incredible jerk, isn't he? No, we taped it this morning. (*Loud gasp.*) Doesn't my nose look gargantuan? Stop humoring me. I have another call. Hold on. (*Clicks phone.*) Hello. Mrs. Stuart? Oh, Mrs. Stuart, the guy hasn't shown up yet. Where is he? Mrs. Stuart, my gold card is garbage now. I need my platinum card. (*SHE picks up a remote control device from the coffee table and hits the mute button, turning off the sound.*)

(*Two shot of Margaret and David. Margaret is wearing a pants suit. David is reading her credits off a cue card. It's obvious.*)

DAVID. "Margaret Thorne Brent. Psychiatrist, author. She returned from London eight months ago to settle here in Windsor Locks. Now her first book is published. A psychological mystery called ... uh, I can't read that, Leslie! I told you to use the Crayolas! Oh, sure! That could be anything!

MARGARET. (*Interrupting.*) It's called *Killing the King.*

Where is this guy? Hold on. (*Clicks phone again.*) Hello? Granville Employment? Where's my cook, Mrs. Johaneston? She didn't show up this morning. I burned my face trying to make toast. Where is she? Hold on please. (*Clicks another button.*) Listen, I have to call you back. I'm talking to American Express and these employment people. My cook is on strike, it seems. 'Bye. (*Clicks phone again.*) Mrs. Stuart? No, IT'S ONLY BEEN A JOINT ACCOUNT FOR SIX MONTHS, NOW, RIGHT? I have all the forms signed

DAVID.
Yeah, thanks.
So. Yeah. Welcome
to my show.

MARGARET.
Thank   you,
David.
DAVID.
Yeah. So, you're
a psychologist?

MARGARET.
Actually,
David. I'm a psychi
...

and ready. Where
IS this guy? You
said seven o'clock.
What? No,that's the
wrong file! – I
DON'T HAVE
ANY CHILDREN.
Hold on, please
(*Clicks the phone
again.*)

Hello? Granville
Employment? Did
you find my cook,
Mrs. Johaneston?
Please don't force
me to make dinner
tonight. It's
JOHANESTON,
you spell it! I don't
know her first
name; it's Hilda, or
Ermgarde, SOME-
THING Nazi. She's
a widow; she lives
alone; it would be
under her name.
Could I speak to
someone else,
please? Thank you.

DAVID.
Okay. And you live here in Windsor Locks?

MARGARET.
Yes. My house was built ...

DAVID.
So, how long have you lived here?

MARGARET.
Eight months.
DAVID.
You British?
MARGARET.
No. Now, in my book ...
DAVID.
Cool. So. You married?
MARGARET.
Yes. My husb ...

DAVID.
So, your real name is Thorne. That's wild, huh?

(Clicks the phone again.)
Mrs. Stuart, did you find him on his little car radio?

(There is a KNOCK at the door.)

He's here now. Thanks. 'Bye. *(Clicks phone again.)* Hello Granville? Could you hold on for a second please? Thank you. (*To door.*) Just a minute (*SHE puts the phone down. Takes American Express forms from desk and moves quickly to the television set, which SHE turns up. SHE then sees the .45 on the chair and puts it on the mantle on her way to open the*

MARGARET.
Killing the ...

DAVID.
Wow. What does
your husband do?

MARGARET.
Also a psychiatrist.
Retired.

DAVID.
Yeah? Is he an old
guy?

*front door. Opens
it. INSPECTOR
JAMES ASCHER is
standing in the
doorway. SHE puts
the forms in his
hand.)*
Here. Tell Mrs.
Stuart she's a
regular guy. (*SHE
goes back to phone.)*
Hello Granville?
Did you find her
number? Elm
Street? (*Slight
pause.*)
I would never want
to VISIT Mrs.
Johaneston, I just
want her number so
I can FIRE her,
Okay? No, buddy,
today is MONDAY.
Can I speak to
someone else,
please? Thank you.

MARGARET.
No, he's been sick.
He has diabetes.

DAVID.
Diabetes. Wow. So,
like, you wrote this
book, huh?

MARGARET.
Killing The King.

DAVID.
Yeah. It's like a
Henry the Eighth
story, right?
MARGARET.
No. That's just a
metaphor ...
DAVID.
It's a murder story.
Right?
MARGARET.
Yes.
DAVID.
Great. And it's very
psychological, huh?
MARGARET.
Yes.

(*To Ascher.*) Oh,
you – you can
double check that in
here. Would you
come in and close
the door please? If
you brought the
cards, I'll sign
them. I ALWAYS
sign for HIM. (*Into
phone.*) Yes, who's
this? Mr. Sanchez.
Mr. Sanchez, if I
could just trouble
you for my cook's
number? You have
no idea how
grateful I could be.
(*To Ascher.*) That's
just a little
interview I taped
this morning. I'll
be right with you.
(*To phone.*) Yes,
Mr. Sanchez. 4966.
I got it. Listen, you
could have her call
me, but not between
eight and eight-
thirty, because I'm
always out
running. Thanks.
(*SHE hangs up.*)

DAVID.
Wow. Lots of clues?
MARGARET.
Yes. but ...
DAVID.
Somebody gets
killed?
MARGARET.
Yes. This woman
kills her husband
DAVID.
Yeah. So how come
a psychologist
knows about
murder? Huh?
Huh?
MARGARET.
The clues in my
book are
psychological ones.
Not conventional.
DAVID.
Wow. Like what,
you mean?

ASCHER.
Mrs. Brent ...
MARGARET.
Just let me watch a
little of this, will
you?
(*MARGARET and
ASCHER watch
TV. MARGARET
laughs.*)
This is sort of a
rehearsal for my
Donahue next
week.

ASCHER.
Oh, yeah?

MARGARET.
Like the way you
keep your legs open
when you talk.
That's a clue,
David. Did you
know that?
DAVID.
Yeah? Like what?
MARGARET.
Well. It's a clue.
About your
personality.
DAVID.
Sure. Like, I'm
very open. Right?

MARGARET.   (*MARGARET*
Maybe. I think you   *switches it OFF.*
keep your legs open *SHE will then roll*
because you know   *the T.V. back into*
you have a big –   *the kitchen.*)

MARGARET. (*Moving to kitchen.*) Pretty
funny stuff, huh? I'll just put this back in the
kitchen. I'm taping it. I'll watch it later. (*Pause.*)
Rather intolerable having to suffer that, but you
see I've never been seriously photographed before.
Well, that's not exactly true. Mother used to
photograph us. Constantly. She found she had no
talent for it. I thought my nose would look bigger
on television. Did it?
ASCHER. No.

MARGARET. (*Has entered the living room and is moving toward her office, picking up the drill on her way.*) You're sweet. But it did look huge. Can I get you a Dewar's or something?

ASCHER. No, I'm ...

MARGARET. (*In office.*) I'm just finishing this bookcase thing. I'll be right with you. (*Sticks her head out of office.*) My husband used to drink scotch. (*Drilling is heard from office.*) If you see any of my husband's guns lying around, please don't fiddle with them. They're probably loaded. Other than that, you have free use of the sitting room.

ASCHER. Uh ... Mrs. Brent ...

MARGARET. (*In office.*) No. Don't talk yet. I'm almost done.

(*ASCHER is standing in front of the fireplace, looking at the painting on the chimney. The DRILLING stops. MARGARET steps into the room from the office.*)

MARGARET. My husband painted that. Seven years ago. As a wedding present.

ASCHER. Oh ...

MARGARET. It's a Harrison Brent original. When we moved here eight months ago from London, he insisted they carefully transfer the bricks. You see? He painted right on the brick.

(*Let me take a moment to describe Harrison's painting. Arid desert. Scorching sun. Man on knees. Shirt sleeves, pants. Tribal man with no face standing over man. The man on his knees has one swiss-cheese arm. Complete with holes. In the bottom left hand corner is a skull. In the top right-hand corner is a dog. Remember: the painting has been done right on the brickface, high above the fireplace opening.*)

ASCHER. Yes. Interesting.
MARGARET. Think so?
ASCHER. Yeah ...
MARGARET. You're much nicer than the other policeman who's been calling me all day. (*Short pause.*)
ASCHER. How did you know I was from the police?
MARGARET. I didn't. At first. May I have those forms back, please?
ASCHER. Oh.

(*ASCHER gives the sheets to Margaret. SHE will put them in the desk, and take out her checkbook to write a check.*)

MARGARET. Thank you. I had a terrible headache this afternoon, and this man named Detective Giarrusso kept calling and asking for my husband. I said I'd take the message. I don't understand why people have to be so cruel. What's *your* name?

ASCHER. Ascher.

MARGARET. Are you a detective?

ASCHER. Technically, I'm an Inspector. How did you know I was from the police?

MARGARET. Because I knew you weren't from American Express.

ASCHER. How did you know I wasn't from American Express?

MARGARET. Your shoes.

ASCHER. What?

MARGARET. Mrs. Stuart told me the man who was coming was driving. As soon as you stepped in I saw all that red Texas mulch from the footpath out back. Q.E.D. Shall I make the check out to the Windsor Locks Police Department?

ASCHER. Check? What check?

MARGARET. Isn't that why you're here? I'm willing to go a hundred dollars. Is that okay?

ASCHER. Mrs. Brent ...

MARGARET. (*Moves to him with the check. Extends.*) Here Go. Wild.

ASCHER. (*Taking check.*) Mrs. Brent, let me expl ...

MARGARET. Call me "doctor." We'll get along better. So, if you don't want this check, what do you want?

ASCHER. I want to see your husband. (*Pause.*)

MARGARET. (*Takes check back, tears it in half.*) He's not here. (*Slight pause.*) Why did you use the foot path?

ASCHER. Never seen the whole house before. It's beautiful. Different.

MARGARET. Thanks.

ASCHER. Do you know when he'll be back?

MARGARET. No. He went out. Walking. He does that every night. For his health. His nerves.

ASCHER. If he does it every night, then you must know when he'll be back.

MARGARET. Only if I know WHEN he left. And I don't.

ASCHER. Did he take the footpath? Because I...

MARGARET. No. He never takes the footpath. He goes through the woods.

ASCHER. Really? At night?

MARGARET. Yes. He loves the woods. He knows the woods.

ASCHER. Still, it would be dangerous ...

MARGARET. I said he knows the woods. (*Pause.*) Maybe I could RELAY the message. It would be very exciting.

ASCHER. No. That's all right. I'll come back tomorrow. Before his walk.

MARGARET. Suit yourself.

ASCHER. Sorry to trouble you.

MARGARET. No trouble. Inspector.

ASCHER. (*Moves to the door.*) Good luck with your book. And the Donahue program next week.

MARGARET. He doesn't practice anymore, y'know.

ASCHER. Pardon?

MARGARET. My husband. He's no longer a practicing psychiatrist. I was just thinking your police force needed a MALE psychiatrist and ...

ASCHER. Mrs. Brent, that's not why I want to see your husband.

MARGARET. Doctor.

ASCHER. It's more of a personal matter. It's not something I can discuss with you. Sorry.

MARGARET. Is it me, or are you just naturally repulsed by aggressive women?

ASCHER. Well. I'll just let myself out. (*HE turns to the door.*)

MARGARET. Should I give him any message?

ASCHER. Just that I'll be by tomorrow. Around seven. (*HE opens the door.*)

MARGARET. Another woman.

ASCHER. Pardon?

MARGARET. That's gotta be it. What, did someone SEE Harrison doing NAUGHTIES in some motel room? Inspector, my husband is a severe diabetic. He never leaves the grounds. I know every move he makes. So why don't you stop playing this game and tell me what you want!

ASCHER. (*Slight pause.*) Doctor. Do you own a red wig? (*Pause.*)

MARGARET. No. Not my style. Why?

ASCHER. I'm following up a report that says your husband was murdered: by a woman of about average height, green dress, red hair. In light of what you just told me, I assume that you must be that woman.

MARGARET. How did I kill him?

ASCHER. (*Pause.*) Gun.

MARGARET. Just blew his little head off?

ASCHER. No. You shot him in the chest. Five times.

MARGARET. If you knew ALL THIS, why did you keep asking to see my husband?

ASCHER. I didn't believe her ...

MARGARET. I'm not answering any more of your questions! I want to call my lawyer! (*She moves to desk and dials phone.*)

ASCHER. That's your right.

MARGARET. Why did you take SO LONG to come around? YOU'RE JUST LOVING THIS! PLAYING SICK GAMES WITH ME! (*To phone.*) Hello, little boy. Would you put your daddy on the phone?

ASCHER. I don't enjoy this, lady.

MARGARET. (*To Ascher.*) Just shuttup! (*To phone.*) COME ON! GET TO THE PHONE!

ASCHER. IT ONLY HAPPENED LAST NIGHT! I had Giarrusso call right away.

MARGARET. (*Has turned her back to Ascher and clicked receiver, hanging up, and then pressed another button. Turning back to him.*) WHAT DID YOU JUST SAY?

ASCHER. (*Long pause.*) I said it only happened last night. (*Pause.*) Oh, Mrs. Johaneston witnessed what happened here last night. She was standing back there.

MARGARET. (*On phone.*) Hello, Phil? It's me. Did I wake you? Listen, Phil, Harrison's dead. Finally. He's been shot. But I need your help. Please don't desert me now, Phil. I love you. I have always loved you. Please say you'll help me. THAT'S RIGHT; YOU GUESSED IT. I'll see you in FIVE minutes. (*SHE hangs up.*)

ASCHER. (*Reading.*) "You have the right to remain silent. Anything you say can and will be used against you in a court of law. You have the right to an attorney. If you give up that right the court will appoint an attorney for you. Do you understand your rights as I have read them to you?"

MARGARET. (*Has crossed to the fireplace.*) What's your first name?

ASCHER. Uh, James. Jim.

MARGARET. Are you married?

ASCHER. Uh. Yes.

MARGARET. (*Taking the gun (.45) off mantle and aiming it at Ascher.*) What did Mrs. Johaneston tell you?

ASCHER. (*Slight pause.*) Put the gun down, Mrs. Brent.

MARGARET. Doctor! Can't you just say "doctor?"

ASCHER. Please ...

MARGARET. You said Mrs. Johaneston made a statement.

ASCHER. (*Slight pause.*) Yes. Mrs. Johaneston made a statement ...

MARGARET. What did she say to you?

ASCHER. I didn't bring the statement with me...

MARGARET. DID YOU TAKE NOTES?

ASCHER. Notes? Yes, right here ...

MARGARET. READ THEM TO ME!

ASCHER. (*Referring to notes.*) Uh ... We thought ... she was nuts ... Uh, Mrs. Johaneston fell asleep in your kitchen .... last night ... She witnessed everything ...

MARGARET. WHAT DID SHE SEE! I WANNA KNOW WHAT SHE SAW!

ASCHER. She saw ... she saw ... Harrison Brent in a tuxedo. Eating ... eating ... eating something. With a gun ... On the phone ... Yelling "How are your British Club friends? ... Did they give you the trophy? I'm using your timers. What a speech you must have made." Then a girl called "Harry" ... I mean yelled "HARRY." Then she heard ANOTHER GIRL'S VOICE saying "I left you one clue." Then the girl with the green dress killed him. That's it.

MARGARET. You should have told me about Mrs. Johaneston when you first came in. Do you see how upset you've gotten me?

ASCHER. Doctor ...

MARGARET. I would have confessed right away ... (*SHE cocks the gun.*)
ASCHER. DON'T COCK THE GUN ... COME ON!

(*MARGARET aims the gun at Ascher's chest.*
A MAN appears on the landing from upstairs.
HE's drying his hair with a towel, so, for the
moment, we can't see his face. The MAN has
no shirt, only slacks. MARGARET sees him.
SHE pulls the trigger. CLICK! No bullets. The
MAN removes the towel from his face. **He is**
the same man we saw in Scene 1. No doubt
whatsoever.)

MAN. I have been looking everywhere for that .45.
MARGARET. (*Lowers the gun.*) Inspector, I'd like you to meet my husband, W. Harrison Brent. Late of London, Pimley's Round Table, Oxford, before that Harvard. Now retired. List of cause: diabetes. Harrison, this is Mr. Ascher.
HARRISON. Jolly good to meet you, old boy ...

(*HARRISON starts to come down to shake hands.*
MARGARET intercepts and interrupts him.
Hands Harrison his .45.)

MARGARET. Here's your toy, Harrison. I must say, your presence in the sitting room when I'm entertaining guests is certainly acceptable.

But I must see a shirt on you, Harrison. DO YOU UNDERSTAND WHAT I'M SAYING? (*Short pause.*)

HARRISON. Oh. Yes. I see. Sorry. Be right back. (*Goes off upstairs.*)

MARGARET. (*Pause.*) Well? Is that the man Mrs. Johaneston saw last night? The one who was shot five times?

(*ASCHER has taken a police artist's rendering of Harrison Brent out of his jacket pocket. It looks exactly like Harrison.*)

ASCHER. Yes. She described him to us.

MARGARET. Hmm. Sure looks like him, doesn't it?

ASCHER. Sure does.

MARGARET. Are you going to arrest me?

ASCHER. (*Slight pause.*) No.

MARGARET. I pulled a gun on you.

ASCHER. Yes, you did.

MARGARET. Well? That's gotta be a crime. Are you all right?

ASCHER. I have to go now. (*Heads for the door.*)

MARGARET. Don't you want a whiskey, or something?

ASCHER. No. My wife will get worried.

MARGARET. Oh. Well. Can't have that.

ASCHER. No.

MARGARET. Goodbye. Drive safely. Or whatever.

(*ASCHER halts at the door. HE walks slowly back to Margaret. HE stands close to her.*)

MARGARET. What is it, dear? Forget something?

(*With his open hand, ASCHER slaps Margaret hard across the face. This flattens her. SHE hits the floor hard. Pause.*)

ASCHER. (*Quietly.*) Goodbye, Mrs. Brent. (*Walks deliberately to the front door.Opens it. Goes out. Closes door. No slam.*
(*MARGARET still on floor. Pause.*)

HARRISON. (*Enters from the landing wearing a shirt and shoes. Sees Margaret. Pause.*) Everything okay?
MARGARET. Go get the keys to the car. We have to go for a ride.
HARRISON. Look here, Margaret ...
MARGARET. GET THE KEYS BEFORE I KILL YOU, SWEETHEART.
HARRISON. Oh. Be right back. (*Exits.*)
MARGARET. (*Pause. Sotto.*) No, sweetheart. Everything is not okay. (*Short pause.*) Not at all.

FADE TO BLACK

Scene 3

Tuesday afternoon. Two-ten. In the blackout we hear a MAN'S VOICE. It is the voice of LIONEL MCAULEY. We will discover that the voice is coming from a cassette player LIONEL is holding.

LIONEL'S VOICE. (*On tape.*) I stop at a dumpster and ditch the gloves, take my mask off. Change clothes. Smile. I hear cop cars but no matter. (*LIGHTS START UP.*) Cops'll never catch me. Never. (*LIONEL shuts tape player off. LIONEL is sitting in the armchair*)

LIONEL. Doctor!

MARGARET. (*Off upstairs.*) Be right down!

LIONEL. My time is valuable!

MARGARET. (*Off.*) Your session begins in one minute, Mr. McAuley!

LIONEL. You don't wear a watch!

MARGARET. (*Off.*) One minute, Mr. McAuley!

LIONEL. Sure. (*Presses record button. Talks softly into tape player.*) I forgot to say how sincerely upset I am over this last one. Much too easy. I just replaced the water for gasoline. Before I cut the hole in his tank. Why are people so stupid? I was sitting in a cafe across from the car when it blew up. I was in disguise. In a dress. It was very symbolic. Me in a dress. Like my wife. Like she was watching her lover blow up in a car. My daughter made the dress for me. A red dress. I've told you this before, doctor. Leave my daughter out of this. She won't tell. She won't tell her mother.

(*STEREO LIGHT goes on. MOZART. MARGARET appears at top of landing. LIONEL shuts off tape player.*)

LIONEL. (*Referring to stereo.*) How did you do that? A timer? Did you use a timer?

MARGARET. Now it's time for our session, Mr. McAuley.

LIONEL. Why do we have to meet here all the time?

MARGARET. My office is here.

LIONEL. You live here.

MARGARET. And work here. All my patients come here.

LIONEL. I never see any of them. Where are they?

MARGARET. All my appointments are staggered. Did you make a new entry in your tape?

LIONEL. No.

MARGARET. No?

LIONEL. Yes. Here. (*Hands her tape.*) Don't listen to it now.

MARGARET. I won't.

LIONEL. You'd better not. You better be alone when you listen to that tape. (*Pause.*) I don't understand the way you had this house built.

MARGARET. What do you mean?

LIONEL. Where are the windows?

MARGARET. I didn't want any. In this room. Except for the skylight.

LIONEL. And what does that say about you?

MARGARET. What do you think it says?

LIONEL. You're hiding something. (*Pause.*) Don't you ever use this fireplace?

MARGARET. Sometimes.

LIONEL. You're lying.

MARGARET. What?

LIONEL. There's no smoke marks in it.

MARGARET. I have it cleaned.

LIONEL. This tray hasn't been used.

MARGARET. It's new.

LIONEL. Where's the screen thingy?

MARGARET. I don't like them.

LIONEL. You're lying.

MARGARET. No, I'm not.

LIONEL. (*Pause.*) I'm developing a theory about this painting. I really am.

MARGARET. Oh?

LIONEL. YES, of course. I go to art exhibits. I've been to the Smithsonian. And to the Louvre.

MARGARET. Have you?

LIONEL. YES I HAVE. I was in Paris for two weeks once. I followed this man named

Richardson all over Paris. You see he once worked for my wife's father. They knew him at the Louvre. He was very popular. For a tall man. Is your husband seeing a psychiatrist?

MARGARET. My husband is a psychiatrist.

LIONEL. I mean, He DID paint THIS, didn't he?

MARGARET. Yes.

LIONEL. He needs help. Immediately. I'm serious.

MARGARET. Why?

LIONEL. Why?? You're so near-sighted, Margaret. It must be your NEW BOOK. Your NEW CAREER has blinded you. Now, the man with the holes in his arm is OBVIOUSLY your husband. And he's trying to get away from the skull and get TO the dog. And this witch doctor person's going to help him. But I still haven't figured out who the witch doctor is. Symbolically, I mean. Although, the position of the dog and the skull is encouraging. I mean, if they were reversed, even an ignoramus could see that your husband was suicidal. But why would somebody switch the bricks? I must be losing my mind. Did you WIN that trophy?

MARGARET. No. It was given to me at a British Club of Hartford, Connecticut banquet about six months ago.

LIONEL. How quaint. (*Short pause.*) I saw you on that David Breuer Show last night.

MARGARET. Did you?

LIONEL. I just said so. My daughter video taped it. You looked interesting.

MARGARET. Thank you.

LIONEL. Your nose looked HUGE.

MARGARET. Really?

LIONEL. You said you once wanted to be a FORENSIC PATHOLOGIST?

MARGARET. Briefly.

LIONEL. I didn't know your husband had diabetes.

MARGARET. Yes.

LIONEL. Serious?

MARGARET. If he breathes near sugar he's a dead man.

LIONEL. If he breathes near sugar he's a dead man? Oh, come on. You're exaggerating.

MARGARET. No. I'm not.

LIONEL. Why don't you just kill him and take his money?

MARGARET. Because the money would go back to his family.

LIONEL. Oh. One of those. I suspected as much.

MARGARET. Did you?

LIONEL. I just said so, didn't I? (*Pause. HE shuts the MUSIC off.*) I go to the theatre now, y'know.

MARGARET. Do you?

LIONEL. I'm off movies. (*Short pause.*) I saw this play last week. It was very bizarre. Very obtuse.

MARGARET. What was it?

LIONEL. I'm telling you. (*Pause.*) These two women live together. With a man. I think they were related. There's a fire escape. He smokes cigarettes out there. (*Pause.*) The older woman had an accent. So did the younger woman. She was the daughter. She was always sad. Good actress. Nice tits. (*Slight pause.*) The man wants to leave. He hates the older woman. She keeps laughing and telling him, "You're not successful. Ha ha ha. You'll never BE successful." He's queer, but he doesn't know it. One of his MALE friends comes over. They smoke cigarettes out on the fire escape. The daughter stays inside. Because she's kind of deformed. She sometimes collects these small glass animals. One of them breaks. (*Slight pause.*) It was a very cruel play. (*Slight pause.*) You know, I think somebody DID switch those bricks.

MARGARET. (*Slight pause.*) Why does your wife cheat on you? (*Pause.*)

LIONEL. Because I want her to.

MARGARET. Why?

LIONEL. (*Close to her.*) Don't get pushy.

MARGARET. Tell me.

(*LIONEL grabs Margaret by the throat pulling her face to his.*)

MARGARET. Let go of me.

LIONEL. Do you realize I could probably tear out one of your eyes with my teeth. Do you realize that?

MARGARET. Let go of me.

LIONEL. (*Lifting Margaret.*) I'm much stronger than you.

MARGARET. I know. (*Pause. LIONEL drops Margaret to floor and runs into kitchen.*)

LIONEL. (*In kitchen.*) Why didn't you call for help? (*Pause.*) You're too small. You're weak. I've known for years she's been cheating on me. HOW DARE YOU ASK ME THAT! (*HE enters.*) I could kill you. Easily. (*HE goes back into the kitchen. Pause.*) This is a very obtuse kind of kitchen. I hate to tell you. (*Pause.*) She keeps leaving me, Margaret. (*Slight pause. HE enters with a box of corn flakes. Pause.*) I must remind you of somebody else. That's the only explanation. I hope you don't mind me having corn flakes – That pastry stuff you put out is much too sweet. It's insulting! I noticed the diplomas in your office. (*HE opens the office door. Looks in.*) Harvard, Johns Hopkins. Margaret Thorne Margaret Thorne. Margaret Thorne Brent. My wife married ME to have children. She's an executive. She's a frequent flyer, if you can believe it. I CAN'T LIVE WITH HER SUCCESS ANYMORE! (*HE slams office door closed.*) What's the matter with you? Do you expect me to just keep talking? Do you think I'm going to just keep talking? Somehow you've concocted this

THEORY about my daughter. **What about** YOUR DAUGHTER? (*Pause.*) **My daughter** is fourteen now. (*Slight pause.*) She's beginning to socialize. She seems to like older men. I don't dance. I did win a science medal in college. **What** a medal. (*Slight pause.*) I plan on giving it **to my** daughter. So she'll never forget me. (*Very **slight** pause.*) And never leave me. I showed her the inscription on my science medal. Even my wife doesn't know what the inscription says. But I showed it to my daughter. Three little words. (*Very slight pause.*) It's our secret.

MARGARET. (*Sotto.*) "Manchester, W.H."

LIONEL. (*Slight pause.*) MANCHESTER, W.H?? You're raving, Margaret! You're not even listening to me! (*Goes in kitchen.*) You know, I've begun following you. (*Slight pause.*) Whenever you come out of your house, I follow you. At night with my car. I know what you've been doing. (*Slight pause, HE enters from kitchen.*) That's why I wrote that letter.

MARGARET. (*Slight pause.*) What letter?

LIONEL. The *letter* I told you about.

MARGARET. What are you *talking* about?

LIONEL. Margaret, I had to protect myself! I mean, I'm in your HOUSE. This isn't an office building. We're five miles from the main road. I HAVE noticed clues. I saw your husband's painting. I saw the fireplace. I saw the David Breuer Show! Do you think I would just WALK down Lakehill Road and into your house without protecting myself first? I wrote a letter to the *New York Times*. (*HE produces an envelope.*) And I'm mailing it today. (*HE puts it back in jacket pocket. Picks up phone. Dials.*) Speaking of which, I want to warn the cab company. I don't want to get stuck here. My wife has my car. Again. Hello. Is this Ace Cab Company? Good. This is Lionel McAuley at 234 Lakehill Road. Yes, me. In ten minutes. The number is 234-1679. You may confirm. (*HE hangs up.*) I can't wait to get home.

MARGARET. (*Very slight pause.*) You say you've been following me?

LIONEL. Yes, I have.

MARGARET. When?

LIONEL. Last night.

MARGARET. Monday night?

LIONEL. Monday night?

MARGARET. Last night – Monday night – You followed me?

LIONEL. Yes, I did.

MARGARET. Where'd I go?

LIONEL. Brenner's Pharmacy. Then to Elm Street. You stopped in front of an apartment building. He stayed seven minutes. You had a MAN in the car with you. He got out. He had a brown bag with him. A LONG THIN BROWN BAG. He went into the apartment building. Then he came back out. Then you pulled away. You went home. Have I answered your question?

(*MARGARET takes trophy from shelf and hits Lionel. HE falls; SHE takes the letter out of his pocket. SHE opens the envelope. IT's empty. LIONEL, from the floor, speaks.*)

LIONEL. So. What are you hiding? (*Pause.*) Can you teach me hypnosis? There's one person I want to hypnotize. (*Slight pause.*) I'm reading your book. It's pretty far-fetched. It's childish. (*Slight pause.*) You didn't even hurt me just now. (*Slight pause.*) Your book is a joke. It's a cheat. The only CRIME committed is through a fantasy. That's cheating. Murder is murder, for Christ's sake. You can't have people getting away with murder just because it's a fantasy. (*Slight pause.*) And there's no such *thing* as the perfect crime. *I* could have told you that. (*Slight pause.*) DO YOU HEAR WHAT I'M SAYING? (*Slight pause.*) Don't you want to play with me anymore?

MARGARET. Do you want to know my favorite fantasy, Lionel?

LIONEL. What?

MARGARET. Murdering my husband.

LIONEL. I knew it.

MARGARET. Let me show it to you. (*Slight pause.*) Let me show you my fantasy. Got a minute?

LIONEL. (*HE looks at his watch.*) Yes.

MARGARET. Go up the stairs. Go down the hallway. My room is the last on the left. In the night table is a gun. Get it. In the walk-in closet next to the bed there's a brown hat box that says Naomi's; get it. Can you remember all that, Lionel?

LIONEL. Sure. Can you remember this? DROP DEAD! HA HA HA HA HA! (*HE runs upstairs laughing.*)

MARGARET. (*Moves the lamp next to the chair and goes to the phone. Sotto on phone.*) Hello, Ace Cab? I'm calling for Mr. McAuley. He would like you to call back here in five minutes, so he'll know to be ready. 234-1679. Thank you. (*Hangs up.*)

LIONEL. (*Appears on the landing. HE has a gun and a hat box.*) Were you just on the phone?

MARGARET. No.

LIONEL. You're lying.

MARGARET. Don't you want to see my fantasy?

LIONEL. You're just trying to break me down.

MARGARET. No, I'm ...

LIONEL. This isn't a game to you! I can read your face very well. What is it you want of me?

MARGARET. Open the hat box. (*SHE turns the LIGHTS down.*)

LIONEL. (*Opens box.*) Whoa, scary.

MARGARET. What's in the box?

LIONEL. Don't you know? (*Takes out a red wig.*)

MARGARET. Good. Now give them to me.

LIONEL. What?

MARGARET. Give me the wig and the gun. I'm going to show you my fantasy.

LIONEL. No way. (*HE puts on the wig. Very slight pause.*) Do I look like a rock star? BUWANG! BUWANG! BUWANG! (*While playing air guitar.*) I have fantasies, too, y'know. Although I haven't written a soon-to-be-bestseller about it. I have my little fantasies.

MARGARET. Tell me.

LIONEL. This gun isn't loaded, is it?

MARGARET. No.

LIONEL. No? (*HE points the gun at her.*)

MARGARET. YES, IT IS LOADED! Lionel, give me the gun!

LIONEL. This is *MY* fantasy. We're on MY time. I'M the patient. (*Holds out the gun.*) I won't point it at you.

MARGARET. Lionel, put the gun in my hand!

LIONEL. Cool out! I know what I'm doing. My wife owns several wigs. (*Slight pause.*) Why did you move the lamp?

MARGARET. I, uh ...

LIONEL. Tell me! (*HE points gun at her.*)

MARGARET. Please, Lionel. I was going to show you how I kill my husband.

LIONEL. Show me.

MARGARET. You're supposed to be in the chair while I'm on the stairs with a green dress, the wig and the gun. So ...

LIONEL. SO, YOU BE ME!

MARGARET. What?

LIONEL. You be me! And I'll be you. Sit down, DOCTOR!

(*SHE sits in the armchair.*)

LIONEL. What happens next? I love this gun.

MARGARET. Well, I ... I come down the stairs.

LIONEL. (*Doing so.*) Saying witty things. I'll wager. Hello, everyone. I'm Doctor Margaret Thorne Brent. Harvard, Harvard, Harvard, Johns Hopkins. Ha, ha ha ha ha. How droll you look. Who are you? It's so dark.

MARGARET. I'm Doctor Brent ...

LIONEL. LIONEL? Is that Lionel? My patient?

MARGARET. No, YOU'RE LIONEL; I'm Doctor Brent ...

LIONEL. No talking while I'm being witty. Oh, Lionel, you're so boring. What do you want from me?

MARGARET. I ...

LIONEL. You want to be cured? You want forgiveness?

MARGARET. Yes.

LIONEL. Forgiveness? For what?

MARGARET. I don't know ...

LIONEL. Can't say?

MARGARET. No ... uh.

LIONEL. What did you do? C'mon, tell me. (*Points gun.*)

MARGARET. LIONEL, PLEASE!

LIONEL. DON'T CALL ME LIONEL!

MARGARET. Please.

LIONEL. Oh, Lionel. What did you do?

MARGARET. MY DAUGHTER. (*Pause.*)

LIONEL. I'll kill you for that! What did you say??

MARGARET. My daughter.

LIONEL. What's that, Lionel? WHAT DID YOU JUST SAY?

MARGARET. I said my daughter.

LIONEL. What did you do to your daughter, Lionel?

MARGARET. I ... (*The PHONE rings.*)

LIONEL. NO. Let it ring, Lionel. (*Points gun.*)

MARGARET. Lionel, let me answer the phone. (*RING.*)

LIONEL. Don't move.

MARGARET. (*Runs screaming to the phone.*) HELP!! HELP!!

LIONEL. NOOOO!

(*HE FIRES GUN. PHONE continues to ring. Pause. HE FIRES again. MARGARET turns and faces him, as though this second shot was the reaction she was looking for.*)

LIONEL. AHHHHHHHHHH!!! (*SHOOTS four more times*)

MARGARET. (*Long pause. Answers phone.*) Hello. (*Slight pause.*) Oh, Ace Cab Company. (*Slight pause.*) Mr. McAuley would like to cancel. (*Slight pause.*) He's decided not to leave yet. (*Slight pause.*) Thank you. (*Hangs up. Pause.*) Come here.

(*LIONEL does.*)

MARGARET. (*Slight pause.*) Sit down.

(*LIONEL does.*)

MARGARET. How do you feel?

LIONEL. (*Slight pause.*) I don't know.

MARGARET. Relax. You look tired. (*Slight pause.*) Relax. (*Slight pause.*) Sleep.

LIONEL. Yes. (*Slight pause.*) I need sleep.

MARGARET. Yes. (*Slight pause.*) You do. (*Slight pause.*) Sleep.

(*A SOPRANO'S VOICE from Mozart's C Minor Mass is heard.*)

FADE TO BLACK

Scene 4

Wednesday night. Eight o'clock.
The SOPRANO has been joined in the darkness
by a CHOIR. After a moment, the LIGHTS
start up.
W. HARRISON BRENT is standing in the
sitting room cleaning a rifle. HE has leisure
clothes on. Very smart. The MUSIC is
playing on the stereo. It is the next night.
HARRISON seems absorbed. After a
moment, there is a KNOCK at the front door.
BRENT continues his task. Now a LOUDER
KNOCK. BRENT looks up.)

HARRISON. I left it unlocked, honey! COME
IN QUICKLY, THOUGH; I FEEL A CHILL!

(The front door opens slowly. We see
INSPECTOR ASCHER. HE comes in. Closes
door. HARRISON is looking at him, pointing
rifle.)

HARRISON. What do you want? Who are
you?
ASCHER. I'M FROM THE POLICE. My
name is Ascher.
HARRISON. Police? (*Puts rifle down. Moves*
to stereo, shuts it OFF.) What's wrong? What's
happened?

ASCHER. Oh, nothing. Nothing, sir. I stopped by to see your wife.

HARRISON. Haven't we met before?

ASCHER. We met the other night.

HARRISON. NO. You look like a doctor friend of mine from Ipswich. England.

ASCHER. We met the other night.

HARRISON. Hmmm? I don't think so. What do you want?

ASCHER. To see your wife.

HARRISON. What? She's not here.

ASCHER. Oh. Do you expect her shortly?

HARRISON. That should be incorrect, shouldn't it? "Expect her shortly?" I'm not sure if one can say that.

ASCHER. I don't ...

HARRISON. She went running. A few minutes ago. Don't know when she'll be back.

ASCHER. Well, I'll just leave her a note ...

HARRISON. You shouldn't really worry about it, you do agree?

ASCHER. Sorry. Worry?

HARRISON. Worry about whether or not your wife has taken a lover. (*Very slight pause.*) You shouldn't. Time you saw a psychiatrist,what?

ASCHER. I came to see Mrs. Brent. I'll leave a note.

HARRISON. She'll be back any minute.

ASCHER. Oh.

HARRISON. Why exactly are you here?

ASCHER. I came to return a cigarette lighter. When I was here the other night, I must have borrowed it, and forgot to return it.

HARRISON. So you've brought it back in good faith. Well done. I'll report your good deed.

ASCHER. I would like ...

HARRISON. Just put it down on the desk and I'll see she gets it.

ASCHER. I would like to get a receipt from you. If you don't mind. (*Very slight pause.*)

HARRISON. Receipt?

ASCHER. (*Very slight pause.*) Yes. (*Slight pause.*)

HARRISON. Margaret handles these things. You'd better wait for her. I don't smoke. Um. Do you want a champagne, or something?

ASCHER. No, thank you. I was admiring your painting the other night.

HARRISON. Were you?

ASCHER. Very ... confusing.

HARRISON. Do you think?

ASCHER. Well ... yeah, sure.

HARRISON. Deliberately confusing, I would say. Painted at a truly desperate time in my life. Since then I have become more SUBTLE about confusing people.

ASCHER. NO IT *IS* CONFUSING. But, I mean ... TO ME ... IT ALMOST MAKES SENSE.

HARRISON. But you need a psychiatrist. I told you that. Nothing to be ashamed of. You MAY sit down, if you like.

ASCHER. Thank you. (*Short pause.*) How did you know about my wife?

HARRISON. What? (*Slight pause.*) Well, it was several things at once, if you get me: your wedding ring, the tie-clip, the shirt collar, lint on your ...

ASCHER. WAIT, YOU LOST ME ...

HARRISON. Your wedding ring's on the wrong hand. Indentation on the LEFT hand is where is SHOULD be. You've started going out at night without it – And why, old boy, is that? Only tonight you've squeezed it back on in a hurry because you're visiting my wife. Stop me if I'm wrong.

ASCHER. The tie-clip.

HARRISON. Well, that's the SAME THING, isn't it? You've turned it face-backwards. Why? Because it's engraved from your wife ...?

ASCHER. Yes, it is!

HARRISON. Building up quite a case against you, aren't we?

ASCHER. What about the shirt collar?

HARRISON. Well, it's not so much the collar as the SHIRT, which is EXPENSIVE, like your tie. Yet you wear ten dollar pants and five dollar shoes. So, you crave expensive things but can only afford half the ensemble. You're a disappointed man, and it's not REALLY that your wife is CHEATING on you, more that she's FINALLY getting out on her own. That's why you've been considering suicide. So, not having slept in two days, you arrive at my house in your best shirt and tie with a receipt and a cigarette lighter saying you must see my wife. Why? Because you're OBSESSED with her. YOU WANT TO FORGET YOUR WIFE AND MAKE MY WIFE YOUR BIG CASE ... (*HE catches himself. Short pause.*) Finally, that spot on your jacket which appears to be lint is actually blue paint from outside the door, where I suspect you've been searching in vain for our jolly old mysterious doorbell. Have I left anything out?

ASCHER. I wasn't aware that you were British.

HARRISON. I'm not. (*Pause.*) Living in London for seven years has a profound effect on the psyche. One simply gets out of bed one morning TALKING BRITISH. Did you say you'd have champagne?

ASCHER. Are you having some?

HARRISON. I will if you will.

ASCHER. Sure.

HARRISON. Splendid. (*In kitchen.*) So, you've got a theory about my painting, eh? Well, let's hear it.

ASCHER. Not really a theory.

HARRISON. (*In kitchen.*) Do you prefer DRY champagne?

ASCHER. Doesn't matter. (*Looking at painting.*) Why the dog? In the painting.

HARRISON. (*In kitchen.*) It's a puppy. Margaret's nickname. Her father used to call her "puppy."

ASCHER. (*Has moved near the painting.*) I think the guy with the holes in his arm is meant to be you. (*Short pause.*)

HARRISON. (*In kitchen.*) I'm listening.

ASCHER. This other person in the painting with no face. Who ...

HARRISON. (*In kitchen.*) Yes, I used to believe that everybody had a Jekyll-and-Hyde personality. What better TWIN to a psychiatrist than a witch doctor, eh? (*Has entered from the kitchen with two glasses.*)

ASCHER. You didn't sign the painting.

HARRISON. Um ... no. Third-rate artists, I believe, have a duty to remain anonymous. (*Holding out glass.*) Well. Here we are. It's rather nice to have some company. (*Hands glass to Ascher.*) Here's to good hunting.

ASCHER. Hunting?

HARRISON. Yes, you know, the dashing inspector stalking that VITAL CLUE. Some people have more than one reason for killing, though. WELL, let's drink.

(*THEY do.*)

ASCHER. I've never tasted champagne like this before. It's so dry.

HARRISON. The only kind I CAN drink, I'm afraid. You see, there is absolutely NO SUGAR in this.

ASCHER. I never knew sugar was in champagne.

HARRISON. Well, natural sugar is everywhere, of course.

(*The front door opens. MARGARET enters, in a running outfit. SHE's out of breath. Her head is down. Holding her sides. SHE doesn't see Ascher at first.*)

HARRISON. I should have brought another glass. We could make a party.

MARGARET. (*Looking up.*) What's going on here?

ASCHER. Uh ... hello ...

HARRISON. Just breaking up the gloom and boredom of everyday life with a little champagne. How was your run? (*Short pause.*)

MARGARET. Have you been waiting to see me, Inspector?

HARRISON. Yes. And I was just ribbing him about being in love with you. He took it awfully well.

MARGARET. (*Short pause.*) Harrison. I have asked you not to bring rifles into this room. Now, pick up the rifle and take it downstairs. I'm not going to tell you this again.

HARRISON. Yes, of course, darling. (*Picks up the rifle. HE will move toward the kitchen.*) I'll just leave you two. Business and all that. The Inspector was kind enough to return a cigarette lighter. I told him I don't smoke. (*Short pause.*) Well, I'm off to the basement. Guns and bullets. What a life. I'll leave my glass. I just wanted a sip. Nice seeing you, Inspector. (*Exits to the kitchen.*)

ASCHER. Same here.

MARGARET. (*Pause.*) What cigarette lighter?

ASCHER. Monday night. When I was here.

MARGARET. You didn't get anywhere near a cigarette lighter. What's going on?

ASCHER. (*Takes the lighter out of his pocket.*) NO, I found it on the footpath out back. This IS your lighter, isn't it?

MARGARET. If it's got a certain little inscription on it. But, then, you must have already looked.

ASCHER. Well, I picked it up ...

MARGARET. Inspector, is there an inscription on the lighter?

ASCHER. Yes ...

MARGARET. Does it say: "To Margaret. With all my love. Phillip"?

(*ASCHER gives the lighter to Margaret.*)

MARGARET. Thank you. I thought I'd lost it. I also appreciate your not showing this to my husband. You're pretty gallant for a one-horse Inspector.

ASCHER. Well ...

MARGARET. Finish the champagne. If you want.

ASCHER. No, I have to be going.

MARGARET. Suit yourself.

ASCHER. If you could just sign this receipt for me.

MARGARET. (*Short pause.*) What receipt?

ASCHER. For the lighter.

MARGARET. I didn't report it missing.

ASCHER. I know. I did.

MARGARET. Fine, YOU sign it.

ASCHER. But, it's your lighter.

MARGARET. DID YOU ASK MY HUSBAND TO SIGN THIS RECEIPT?

ASCHER. Uh, yah ...

MARGARET. What's going on here, Ascher? What are you up to? (*Moving to phone.*) Maybe I should call your Commissioner ...

ASCHER. NO, C'MON! I'M NOT SUPPOSED TO BE HERE!

MARGARET. Will you tell me WHAT THE HELL IS GOING ON?

ASCHER. I was dreaming about Sunday night, when you shot your husband; y'know, when Mrs. Johaneston saw you in the green dress? That was you in the green dress on Sunday night, right?

MARGARET. Yes.

ASCHER. Only in my DREAM, your husband REALLY DIED and you got this OTHER GUY to take his place.

(*MARGARET starts to laugh.*)

ASCHER. No, I thought it was crazy too, but then I remembered the signatures.

MARGARET. (*Pause.*) What signatures?

ASCHER. The ones on the American Express form you handed me. Oh, I'm the Windsor County handwriting expert. I testify at trials.

MARGARET. I'm so happy.

ASCHER. No, I've been thinking about this for two days. It's a puzzle.

MARGARET. Maybe you oughtta sit down.

ASCHER. Like that painting. You look at it and you feel that something's wrong.

MARGARET. Tell me about the signatures.

ASCHER. I need three chairs. To explain it. Folding chairs if you've got 'em.

MARGARET. Ummm. I have group analysis folding chairs. Do they count?

ASCHER. Sure.

MARGARET. If I get you these chairs will you tell me about the signatures?

ASCHER. That's why I need the chairs.

MARGARET. I'll get them. (*SHE goes into office.*)

ASCHER. Thanks. (*Slight pause.*) Your husband was just telling me that your father used to call you "puppy."

MARGARET. (*In office.*) My husband used to call me "puppy," too.

ASCHER. Oh. (*Slight pause.*) God, what a week.

MARGARET. (*In office.*) Do you have a heavy case load?

ASCHER. I wish I did. I trained for Homicide. But there's only been one murder in this town in the last five years. So, I've been assigned to every department.

MARGARET. (*In office.*) Oh? What murder?

ASCHER. Six months ago. We fished a young girl of about eighteen, or twenty out of Scotty's Pond.

MARGARET. (*In office.*) Drowned?

ASCHER. No. Whoever killed her, DRUGGED her, BEAT her to death, then threw the body in the pond.

MARGARET. (*Standing in the office entrance way. SHE is holding three folding chairs under her arms.*) You never caught the killer?

ASCHER. We couldn't even identify the dead girl. She's still listed as Jane Doe. Body found naked. Head beaten in. Good looking girl. Was. SHE was a redhead.

MARGARET. (*Slight pause.*) Here are your folding chairs.

ASCHER. (*Short pause.*) This is very nice of you. I mean. HUMORING me like this. Look, I know you pulled a gun on me and I know I hit you, but ...

MARGARET. Tell me about the signatures.

ASCHER. Okay. Now, if you remember Monday night, you'll remember that you handed me that folder. Because you thought I was the American Express guy.

MARGARET. I remember.

ASCHER. (*Opens two of the folding chairs and stands them near each other.*) These two chairs will represent the two signatures I saw on the American Express form. (*HE looks around the room.*) I'm gonna put this tray of pastry on this chair to represent YOUR HUSBAND's signature. (*HE does.*) And this trophy on the other to represent YOUR signature. (*HE does.*) What *is* that? – (*Reads inscription on trophy.*) "The British Club of Hartford Connecticut"?

MARGARET. Ascher. Get on with this. I'm tired.

ASCHER. Sorry. Okay. Your signature. Your husband's signature.

MARGARET. That's it?

ASCHER. No. Then there was the THIRD signature. (*HE will set up the third chair AWAY from the two.*)

MARGARET. (*Slight pause.*) WHAT THIRD SIGNATURE?

ASCHER. (*Very slight pause.*) Remember when you wrote that check: on Monday night, when you thought I'd come for a donation?

MARGARET. Oh, right.

ASCHER. I SAW the signature on the check before you tore it up.

MARGARET. (*Very slight pause.*) So?

ASCHER. You signed your HUSBAND'S NAME on the check.

MARGARET. LIKE I ALWAYS DO.

ASCHER. That's what I thought: because your husband's signature on the CHECK, and your husband's signature on the AMERICAN EXPRESS FORM MATCHED EXACTLY: so you must have signed BOTH.

MARGARET. Obviously.

ASCHER. But here's the problem: YOUR SIGNATURE DIDN'T MATCH THE OTHER TWO. (*Slight pause.*) IT SHOULD'VE.

MARGARET. Inspector, since I always sign for him, did it ever occur to you that when my signature is required next to his, I'm certainly not going to sign MY OWN NAME.

ASCHER. So, you must have had your husband sign for you.

MARGARET. LIKE HE ALWAYS HAS.

ASCHER. (*Very slight pause.*) LIKE HE ALWAYS HAS. So, you would *never* have let the PHONY GUY sign the form.

MARGARET. (*Slight pause.*) Have you fixated on me, Ascher?

ASCHER. (*Very slight pause.*) What?

MARGARET. Look, if you need psychiatric help, say so. A lot of mentally unbalanced cops ...

ASCHER. HOW DARE YOU TALK TO ME LIKE THAT!! WHO THE HELL DO YOU THINK YOU'RE TALKING TO?

MARGARET. That's it, I've had enough!

ASCHER. YOU GONNA PULL A GUN ON ME AGAIN?

MARGARET. YOU LOOKED PRETTY SCARED THE LAST TIME I DID!

ASCHER. I KNOW YOU'VE MURDERED YOUR HUSBAND! (*Slight pause.*) And you know I can't prove anything. If I could have gotten that man's signature, I would've had something to take to the Commissioner. BUT I'LL THINK OF SOMETHING ELSE!

MARGARET. I didn't mean to get you so upset. I'm sorry. Would you excuse me. (*Moving toward kitchen.*) HARRISON! Harrison? Could you come up here, please? (*To Ascher.*) Are you sure you don't want to finish your champagne?

ASCHER. No. Thank you.

MARGARET. What if I were to let him SIGN your receipt?

ASCHER. (*Slight pause.*) You'd never do that.

MARGARET. Why not?

ASCHER. I'd know he was a phony.

MARGARET. But you couldn't prove it.

ASCHER. But I'd know I was right.

MARGARET. So what?

ASCHER. I could tell the Commissioner.

MARGARET. Based on a signed receipt?

HARRISON. (*Enters.*) How can I help?

MARGARET. Harrison. Would you be a dear and sign MY NAME on the Inspector's receipt before he suffers any more brain damage?

HARRISON. (*To Ascher.*) Be glad to. Got a pen?

ASCHER. Uh ... yah ... sure.

HARRISON. Let's do it at the desk. Best to be neat, eh?

MARGARET. I always feel a good host should at least SOUND British.

(*HARRISON had moved to the desk. So has ASCHER. ASCHER hands pen to Harrison.*)

ASCHER. Just sign anywhere.

HARRISON. Anywhere?

ASCHER. Right there.

(*HARRISON signs. ASCHER looks on. HARRISON hands pen back to Ascher. HARRISON heads back toward kitchen.*)

HARRISON. If that will be all, I'd like to get back to my sub-machine gun.

MARGARET. Thank you, dear.

(*HARRISON exits, closing the kitchen door behind him. ASCHER is staring at the receipt. HE recognizes the signature.*)

MARGARET. Have you solved the murder, Inspector Ascher?

ASCHER. I'm sorry to have wasted your time. I'll go. (*HE restores the room. To himself.*) Get the signature.I don't know.

MARGARET. You all right?

ASCHER. Lately I've been thinking about my job. I don't really have one. Please don't tell the Commissioner I was here.

MARGARET. Not a word.

ASCHER. He'd fire my ass.

MARGARET. Don't worry, I won't.

ASCHER. Good night.

MARGARET. Good night.

(*The PHONE rings.*)

ASCHER. I'll let myself out.

(*The PHONE rings again. ASCHER is opening the door. MARGARET answers the phone.*)

MARGARET. (*To phone.*) Yes. (*Short pause.*) Yes he is. Hold on. (*To Ascher.*) It's for you. It's your Detective Giarrusso.

ASCHER. (*Moving to the phone.*) Oh. I told him I was here. Thank you.

(*SHE sits on the couch, reading a magazine.*)

ASCHER. (*On phone.*) Yah. What is it? (*Pause.*) When? (*HE has his notebook and pen out. Pause.*) Who called it in? Are you saying ELM Street? (*Short pause.*) What'd the coroner say? (*Short pause.*) TELL HIM I'M IN CHARGE OF THIS CASE! (*Short pause.*) Ten minutes. (*HE hangs up, staring at the receipt again.*) Your cook. Mrs. Johaneston. Is dead.

MARGARET. (*Looking up.*) How?

ASCHER. Someone beat her head in with a blunt instrument.

MARGARET. (*Short pause.*) Poor woman. (*SHE goes back to reading.*)

ASCHER. (*Moves to the front door. Opens it.*) Oh, Mrs. Brent.

MARGARET. Doctor.

ASCHER. I'll be back.

(*ASCHER goes out. Closes door. Pause. The kitchen door opens slowly. HARRISON steps out. Pause.*)

HARRISON. He's not going to give up. (*Slight pause.*)

MARGARET. I know. (*Slight pause.*) He almost had it figured out. He has the time frame wrong, though.

HARRISON. (*Pause.*) He's in love with you.

MARGARET. (*Slight pause.*) I continued hypnotizing Lionel today. (*Slight pause.*) The police will believe he's the killer.

HARRISON. What if they break him down?

MARGARET. (*Very slight pause.*) But he is a killer. (*Slight pause.*) I told him about Carlotta Donovan.

HARRISON. Why?

MARGARET. Because I needed to talk about it again. I ...

HARRISON. BUT ASCHER SAID THEY NEVER IDENTIFIED THE BODY!

MARGARET. You always trivialize our discussions – I wasn't talking about her BODY, I was talking about her as a PATIENT. WHY did she come here that night? WHY did she say those things on the tape? WHAT CLUE DID SHE LEAVE ME? (*Very slight pause.*) Listen, why don't you go to the guest house? I want to work for awhile. I have to think. Okay?

HARRISON. I love you.

MARGARET. (*Very slight pause.*) Tell me we're not gonna get caught.

HARRISON. (*Very slight pause.*) They'll never figure out why Mrs. Johaneston was killed.

MARGARET. (*Very slight pause.*) We'll see.

(*HE exits through the kitchen. MARGARET stands there. Pause.*)

SLOW FADE TO BLACK

END OF ACT I

ACT II

Scene 5

Friday night. Nine o'clock.
We hear Mozart. From the String Quartet in C
Major. Stage LIGHTS start up. The sitting
room of the Brent home. Two nights later. The
music is now coming from the stereo.
Skylight. MOON. The kitchen LIGHT is on.
We hear GLASS BREAK in the office. We
hear NOISE in the office We see the office
LIGHT go on. LIONEL comes out of the office.
HE's dressed in dark clothes. HE moves to
stereo. SHUTS it off. HE stands staring at the
painting. MARGARET enters from kitchen.

MARGARET. Lionel, what are you doing
here?!

LIONEL. Y'know, that witch doctor is driving
me crazy.

MARGARET. Lionel!

LIONEL. I broke in at your office. I'll pay for
the glass. I didn't think you'd let me in.

MARGARET. (*Moving toward the office.*) I
don't even think you should be here ...

73

LIONEL. You never told me there was a GUEST HOUSE on the premises. It's all lit up. There's a man over there. Reading.

MARGARET. (*SHE stops.*) I know.

LIONEL. The same man I saw in the car. When I followed you on Monday night.

MARGARET. Yes.

LIONEL. Yes. (*Slight pause.*) He went into that old woman's apartment building on Elm Street. With a long brown bag. I witnessed that.

MARGARET. Li ...

LIONEL. Does he love you? (*HE grabs her.*) You're giving yourself away with these STUPID CLUES! Don't you realize that? Margaret, – you don't have to keep hypnotizing me. I'm not deranged. I WANT TO GET CAUGHT! I'm not like you. I DON'T WANT MY DAUGHTER TO SUFFER ANYMORE! (*Pause. HE lets go of her.*) I definitely remind you of someone else. (*Short pause.*) Why did you tell me about Carlotta Donovan? You know, if you'd only let me listen to that tape, maybe I could help. (*Slight pause.*) DID YOU KILL HER, TOO? (*A KNOCK at the door.*) Don't worry. I'll go out through the office window.

MARGARET. (*Sotto.*) No. Take the footpath. This way. It's two miles to the road. (*SHE leads HIM to the kitchen door.*)

LIONEL. I must see you tomorrow! I'll kill myself if I don't!

MARGARET. Fine, now go!

LIONEL. (*Sotto.*) Oh. I'm learning to dance, by the way.

MARGARET. (*Sotto.*) GO! (*SHE pushes him out the kitchen door and HE is gone. To front door.*) Just a minute! (*SHE closes office door, then moves to the front door, and throws it open. ASCHER is standing in the doorway.*)

MARGARET. I thought you would've FOUND the doorbell by now. Shame on you.

ASCHER. (*Looking around doorway.*) There's no doorbell out here!

MARGARET. It's well hidden. For the mysteriously inclined. Will you come in and close the door?

ASCHER. (*Comes in. Closes door.*) Am I disturbing you?

MARGARET. No. I was upstairs, finishing some work. How are you?

ASCHER. Very well. Thank you.

MARGARET. You look well. Murder cases must agree with you.

ASCHER. I don't know about that ...

MARGARET. This is an official visit? Yes?

ASCHER. Sort of. Yes.

MARGARET. Do you need my husband for this? (*SHE picks up phone, as if to call him.*)

ASCHER. Uh, not right now. Where is he?

MARGARET. He's at the guest house. Reading.

ASCHER. Guest house?

MARGARET. Out back. Beyond the woods. I thought you'd snooped all over my property.

ASCHER. No.

MARGARET. So, make with the questions already.

ASCHER. (*Has his notebook and pencil out. We many notice some bulky object in one of his jacket pockets.*) Mrs. Johaneston worked for you ... how long?

MARGARET. Not quite two weeks.

ASCHER. And her job ...

MARGARET. She was a cook. She cooked.

ASCHER. But her SCHEDULE ...

MARGARET. Breakfast, mainly. Sometimes dinner.

ASCHER. Like Sunday night.

MARGARET. Like Sunday night.

ASCHER. When did you last see her?

MARGARET. Sunday night.

ASCHER. You didn't try to call her on Monday?

MARGARET. No.

ASCHER. You didn't visit her?

MARGARET. I don't know where she lives. (*Slight pause.*)

ASCHER. (*Referring to his notebook.*) Uh ... that's not true. You were yelling at the employment people on Monday night. They kept giving you her address and you wanted the phone number.

MARGARET. I didn't visit her.

ASCHER. Okay.

MARGARET. Why is Monday night so important?

ASCHER. That's when she was killed. Monday night. (*Short pause.*) She lived alone. The super finally kicked the door down. That's why it took us two days to find out.

MARGARET. And the killer used a baseball bat?

ASCHER. How did you know that?

MARGARET. I have several newspapers delivered.

ASCHER. Right.

MARGARET. Any more questions?

ASCHER. Did you like her?

MARGARET. Off the record?

ASCHER. Sure.

MARGARET. Hated her.

ASCHER. Why?

MARGARET. (*Short pause.*) She was a sneak. She was the town gossip. (*Very slight pause.*) Could repeat entire conversations upon request. Am I counting the ways?

ASCHER. What about your patients?

MARGARET. They hated her, too.

ASCHER. I think you know what I'm getting at.

MARGARET. You want to know if one of my patients is crazy enough to have killed her.

ASCHER. That's right.

MARGARET. Is that a court order in your pocket?

ASCHER. No.

MARGARET. Then don't ask me questions about my patients.

ASCHER. Okay. That's it. (*Putting notebook away*.)

MARGARET. Really? Aren't you gonna GRILL me, or DRILL me, whatever you people do?

ASCHER. No.

MARGARET. So. Got any hot leads?

ASCHER. A couple.

MARGARET. Good. (*Short pause.*) You look good.

ASCHER. Thank you. So do you.

MARGARET. Right.

ASCHER. Right. Well, good night.

MARGARET. Good night.

ASCHER. Listen, thanks again.

(*Pause. THEY are close to each other. Very quickly, ASCHER takes Margaret in his arms. THEY kiss. Pause. HE's still holding her.*)

ASCHER. I couldn't stop thinking about you.

MARGARET. Don't say too much.

ASCHER. I know.

MARGARET. You shouldn't be kissing suspects, anyway.

ASCHER. You're not a suspect. (*Slight pause.*)

MARGARET. I'm not?
ASCHER. No.

(*SHE kisses him. Short pause. SHE moves away from him.*)

MARGARET. Do you want a drink? Do you have time?
ASCHER. Um. Sure. Are you drinking?
MARGARET. I may have a belt. You like Scotch? I got some Johnny Black.
ASCHER. Sure. I'll take it straight up.
MARGARET. What a guy.

(*SHE moves to the liquor cabinet. SHE will prepare two drinks. ASCHER takes a hardcover book out of his jacket pocket. The book is* Killing the King, *by Margaret Thorne Brent.*)

ASCHER. I finished your book.
MARGARET. You CAN sit down, y'know.
ASCHER. Thank you. (*HE sits.*)
MARGARET. So. About the book.
ASCHER. I liked it a lot.
MARGARET. I'm glad.
ASCHER. Very psychological.
MARGARET. (*Very slight pause.*) Yah. Well, the first draft was all about PLUMBING, but I figured HEY, YOU'RE NOT A PLUMBER, so I

put all the psychology stuff back. Here's your
drink. (*SHE has a drink also.*)

ASCHER. You look very pretty today.

MARGARET. Don't. Let's drink. (*THEY do.*)
I gotta have ice. Excuse me. (*SHE goes in the
kitchen.*) If those shoes are killing you, you can
take them off.

ASCHER. (*Short pause.*) Thanks.

MARGARET. (*In kitchen.*) It seems illogical
that policemen don't wear sneakers.

ASCHER. (*Taking his shoes off.*) Well ...
there's a reason ...

MARGARET. (*In kitchen.*) Tell me about the
book.

ASCHER. I liked it. There's one passage in it
that I particularly enjoyed.

MARGARET. (*In kitchen.*) The chapter on
sexual fantasies.

ASCHER. No. The passage in the chapter on
MURDER.

MARGARET.(*In kitchen.*) Oh. Did you like
that chapter?

ASCHER. Very much. There's NO WAY that
girl could get a loaded gun away from a cop.

MARGARET. (*In kitchen.*) I disagree.

ASCHER. No way. The cop would have
known her plan. He would never have put real
bullets in that gun.

MARGARET. (*In kitchen.*) I thought you
LIKED this book.

ASCHER. I do. Can I read this one passage?

MARGARET. (*In kitchen.*) Oooh, Mr. Ascher, WOULDYA??

ASCHER. Sure.

(*ASCHER opens the book. Thumbs. The kitchen LIGHT is switched off. MARGARET enters from the kitchen. Carrying a glass of ice. SHE turns the overhead LIGHT DOWN.*)

MARGARET. Do you mind if I turn some music on?

ASCHER. (*Looking through book.*) Go ahead.

MARGARET. I'm in a Friday night mood. And it needs music. (*SHE has reached the stereo. Turns on the radio. JAZZ. Smoky sax.*)

ASCHER. Here it is. Ready?

MARGARET. You bet. (*SHE sits in the armchair.*)

ASCHER. (*Reading from book.*) "You must commit the crime so no one can tell a crime has been committed. Yes. She agreed. To her, THAT was what the perfect crime was. Slowly, the idea was coming. She was thinking of her husband. She was thinking of murder." (*Closes the book.*)

MARGARET. That's ridiculous.

ASCHER. Pardon?

MARGARET. There's only one crime I know of that you could CONCEIVABLY commit perfectly.

ASCHER. What's that?

MARGARET. Suicide.

ASCHER. (*Short pause.*) Could I have some of this cake? Scotch makes me hungry.

MARGARET. Help yourself. Murder sells. For some reason.

ASCHER. (*Eating.*) Mmm.

MARGARET. There's a chicken in the refrigerator, if you're hungry.

ASCHER. This is fine. Did you bake this?

MARGARET. Sara Lee did. (*Slight pause.*) How old are you, Ascher?

ASCHER. Thirty-eight.

MARGARET. I'm thirty-six. Don't I look it? (*Very slight pause.*) How's your wife?

ASCHER. (*Short pause.*) She's good.

MARGARET. Is she happy about your new murder case?

ASCHER. Not really.

MARGARET. Why not?

ASCHER. She's not interested in police work.

MARGARET. Really. Do you have any children?

ASCHER. No. We can't have children. (*Short pause.*) She wants to be an actress. I think.

MARGARET. Really.

ASCHER. Lately, she does. (*Short pause.*) She likes going to Dunkin Donuts with actors. Y'know? (*Slight pause.*) You don't have any children, do you? I mean, I didn't think you did. Do you? Have any children?

MARGARET. No. I don't. (*Pause.*) I HAD
one, once. (*Pause.*) I had to ... give it up. (*Pause.*)
So, no. I don't have any children.

ASCHER. (*Very slight pause.*) Can I ask you
a question about your sexual fantasies?

MARGARET. (*Smiles. Kisses him.*) Ask.

ASCHER. What were you doing with your
husband last Sunday night? I mean, what was all
that stuff that Mrs. Johaneston SAW? You know
when you were in the green dress with the wig and
the guns.

MARGARET. Yes.

ASCHER. I mean, it if WAS just kinky sex,
you can say so.

MARGARET. Harrison was helping me with
a problem.

ASCHER. I don't understand.

MARGARET. Well, you read my book. Part
of my methodology is to have patients ACT OUT
their fantasies or nightmares.

ASCHER. Psychodrama?

MARGARET. Sort of. And since this patient
is no longer around, and since HER problem is
still MY problem, I asked Harrison to give me a
hand. We didn't know the old bag was
WATCHING.

ASCHER. So, Mrs. Johaneston saw you
ACTING OUT SOME GIRL'S DREAM.

MARGARET. Some girl's NIGHTMARE.

ASCHER. Why?

MARGARET. Why what?

ASCHER. Why ACT IT OUT?

MARGARET. Oh. To try to see the nightmare from her point of view. It's kind of like RE-CREATING THE SCENE OF A CRIME.

ASCHER. Oh! And you REHEARSE this often? With your husband?

MARGARET. Yes. I have to have it EXACT.

ASCHER. So. This girl has a dream about shooting your husband.

MARGARET. No. I told you. Harrison was pretending to be somebody else.

ASCHER. And YOU were pretending to be HER.

MARGARET. Right.

ASCHER. Can you tell me the dream?

MARGARET. (*Slight pause.*) Why do you want to know?

ASCHER. You said it was a problem. Maybe I can help

MARGARET. You're funny, Ascher. See, when people dream, they dream in LAYERS. Let's say your wife buys a new dress, the mailman cuts himself on your fence, a Frank Sinatra song comes on while you're shaving; all this could become one nightmare when you go to sleep.

ASCHER. The mailman looks like Frank Sinatra.

MARGARET. Right, or he's wearing your wife's dress. My problem with this girl's dream is it doesn't appear to be layered.

ASCHER. I don't understand.

MARGARET. Neither do I. (*Short pause.*) Actually, I was thinking about her today. She had blazing red hair. She just appeared on my doorstep one day. I don't know who gave her my name. Want some more Scotch?

ASCHER. No, go ahead.

MARGARET. (*Pause. Now on her feet.*) Okay. The basic stuff you should know going in is that she had been sexually abused. By her stepfather. She was adopted. Originally from England – Cockney – over here on a scholarship. She said. The nightmare begins with a clock chiming ten. A strange man in a tuxedo enters a room.

ASCHER. Your husband.

MARGARET. No. The man has no face. Think of my husband as an ACTOR.

ASCHER. Okay—he "enters" the room—

MARGARET. Right—

ASCHER. THIS room?

MARGARET. Yes. He looks at his watch. Rock music starts playing: it has a HARD BEAT—

ASCHER. How do you do that?

MARGARET. Do what?

ASCHER. Make the rock music go on.

MARGARET. (*Quickly.*) Timers. I use timers. Can I continue?

ASCHER. Go ahead.

MARGARET. The man has gloves on. He walks directly to my office door, throws it open, turns the light on. A woman's voice begins speaking from inside my office.

ASCHER. Tape recorder, right?

(Slight pause.)

MARGARET. Right.

ASCHER. GIRL's voice, right? Not WOMAN's voice.

MARGARET. *(Quickly.)* She'd vacillate, though: sometimes she'd say it was her voice, sometimes MY voice.

ASCHER. But when you act it out with your husband—

MARGARET. *(Interrupting.)* Sometimes I use HER voice, sometimes MY voice—

ASCHER. *(Interrupting.)* But last Sunday night, you used HER voice.

MARGARET. *(Quickly.)* Right.

ASCHER. And ANOTHER timer.

MARGARET. What are you getting at?

(Pause.)

ASCHER. I'm not getting at anything. Go ahead.

(Slight pause.)

MARGARET. The man begins searching my desk. He finds a gun. He moves to this chair, sits, picks up a magazine, pretends to read it.

ASCHER. The voice in the office is still speaking?

MARGARET. Yes. And it's saying terrible things: "I've never loved you. I've betrayed you." And just as it says "I hate you" a girl with red hair in a green dress appears on the landing.

ASCHER. That's HER, right?

MARGARET. (*Lost.*) Who?

(*Slight pause.*)

ASCHER. Your patient.

(*Slight pause.*)

MARGARET. She could never see the girl's face. (*Slight pause.*) She said it could be me in disguise.

(*Slight pause.*)

ASCHER. Why is the dress GREEN?

MARGARET. Money.

(*Slight pause.*)

ASCHER. I don't understand.

(Slight pause.)

MARGARET. If the girl in the green dress is HER, it symbolizes an obsession with money: she used to wear these cheap clothes, terrible perfume.

ASCHER. What if the girl is you?

(Pause.)

MARGARET. *(Slowly.)* If the girl is ME, it means, for some unknown reason, she hated me.

(Pause.)

ASCHER. What happens next?

(Pause.)

MARGARET. The man cocks the gun, stands up quickly. Suddenly, another gun appears in her hand, SHE FIRES. He STAGGERS toward my office, she keeps firing. He's inside the office. She stops in the doorway. He's dead. *(Slight pause.)* The voice in the office has stopped speaking. She goes in. Closes the door. *(Slight pause.)* She wakes up. *(Pause.)* I could've prevented this.

(Pause.)

ASCHER. Prevented what?

(Pause.)

MARGARET. Her going away. *(Slight pause.)* I was so OBSESSED with finishing my book, getting it published, I WASN'T LISTENING. I was so smug with her, I ...

(Pause.)

ASCHER. Why do you keep acting out the nightmare?

(Slight pause.)

MARGARET. There's something missing. One piece, one FACT I don't know. *(Pause.)* ANYWAY THAT'S what Mrs. Johaneston saw last Sunday night: ME WORKING.

(Pause.)

ASCHER. Could I have some more Scotch?
MARGARET. It's over there. Get it.

(ASCHER moves to cabinet.)

MARGARET. You can pour.
ASCHER. *(While pouring.)* When did you receive this trophy from the British Club?

MARGARET. Umm. I don't remember. About six months ago. Let's sit on the sofa. (*Short pause.*)

ASCHER. Okay. (*HE does.*)

MARGARET. You know, you have a nice nose.

ASCHER. Yeah? Thank you. So do you.

MARGARET. Yeah? Well, you're a lyin' fool How about that?

ASCHER. I think you're very attractive.

MARGARET. Kiss me. (*THEY kiss. SHE pulls away.*) So how come you wanna know about my fantasies?

ASCHER. Curious.

MARGARET. Uh huh. Are you falling in love with me, Ascher?

ASCHER. (*Slight pause.*) Yes.

MARGARET. So, how come I'm not a suspect?

ASCHER. (*Short pause.*) Because you had no reason for killing Mrs. Johaneston.

MARGARET. (*Very slight pause.*) Did you ever taste her sauerbraten?

ASCHER. There's one OTHER thing we haven't told the press. Yet.

MARGARET. What's that?

ASCHER. You remember Jane Doe? That girl I told you about we fished out of Scotty's Pond six months ago?

MARGARET. Your only unsolved murder. I remember.

ASCHER. Whoever killed Mrs. Johaneston, killed Jane Doe. We're positive.

MARGARET. (*Very slight pause.*) How do you know?

ASCHER. (*Very slight pause.*) Both women had the letter A carved into their foreheads with a knife.

MARGARET. (*Very slight pause.*) That'll do it. (*Slight pause.*)

ASCHER. A for adulteress.

MARGARET. So, are you going to make a heavy PASS at me, or are you waiting for me to JUMP on you?

ASCHER. I ... I didn't know ... what you wanted.

MARGARET. (*SHE leans close to him.*) Keep your hands by your sides. Let me do this. Don't talk. (*SHE undoes his tie. Opens his shirt.*)

ASCHER. Margaret.

MARGARET. Be quiet.

ASCHER. Tell me who PHILLIP is.

MARGARET. (*Pause. SHE slowly pulls away from him.*) Why don't you tell me about your Commissioner?

ASCHER. What? What do you want to know about him?

MARGARET. Well. I read in the paper today that he's on the verge of arresting this baseball bat killer.

ASCHER. Yah, right.

MARGARET. I thought this was YOUR case.

ASCHER. Oh, come on, Mrs.Brent. You said you read the newspaper. It's *his* case now. I'm just doing the legwork. He's got seven county police departments combing the woods for a psychopathic killer. Still, he looks good on the six o'clock news. With his thousand dollar suits. (*Slight pause.*) What's HE worth?

MARGARET. Who?

ASCHER. Your husband. How much money does he have?

MARGARET. Two hundred million.

ASCHER. Where did you meet him? School?

MARGARET. Yes. At Harvard.

ASCHER. YOU didn't come from money, though, did you?

MARGARET. Does it show that much?

ASCHER. You were poor.

MARGARET. My father blew his brains out. And then we were poor.

ASCHER. OH.

MARGARET. I DID win my scholarship, which cheered me up.

ASCHER. Which is where you met Harrison Brent.

MARGARET. Right.

ASCHER. And fell in love.

MARGARET. Hardly, (*Pause.*) What I wanted was to be the greatest psychiatrist who ever lived.

ASCHER. And what happened?

MARGARET. I just told you. My father killed himself. If you were a woman you'd understand. You take your strength for granted. It's not like that for a woman. My father was my strength—until a month before I left for Harvard. He went into his den and shot himself.

ASCHER. Why?

MARGARET. Money. Pride. But hey, I thought you wanted to know who Phillip was.

ASCHER. Oh, right.

MARGARET. It's funny; my first month at Harvard was spent DOGGING Harrison Brent.

ASCHER. Really?

MARGARET. Oh yeah, this guy wanted me badly. I was on a work-study program, working in the library. Harrison used to breeze in with several society buddies, demanding books way up in the stacks; they liked watching me climb the ladder. And I wore these horrible black dresses that whole month. It's not like I was baiting him. Harrison called my dorm incessantly; he kept leaving me little notes. All the girls thought I was nuts for evading him, but I kept ... (*Pause.*) I kept holding onto a greatness I had. When my father was alive. He believed in me. That was the whole thing. But it was slipping away. How could he betray me like that? He never talked to me about it.

ASCHER. How could he talk to you about it? He knew you needed his strength. How could he show you that side?

MARGARET. (*After a pause.*) So Harrison keeps calling my dorm, leaving me notes in the library. Finally, he invites me to the Harvard Annual Halloween Costume Ball. And guess what?

ASCHER. You say yes.

MARGARET. I say yes.

ASCHER. What was your costume?

MARGARET. Lizzie Borden. It was a big hit. Harrison was Zorro.

ASCHER. Yeah?

MARGARET. Yeah, you know how the British are: they love all that dress-up, with big hats, capes ...

ASCHER. He told me he wasn't British.

MARGARET. Harrison? He was pulling your leg. His family OWNS England. Where was I?

ASCHER. Costume Ball.

MARGARET. Right. So the night of the Ball, my mother sends me a telegram: "Wealthier than God. Stop. Family controls money. Keep him alive. Love, Mother." So I get to the Ball. Harrison's trotting me around, introducing me to all his filthy-rich friends. The place is packed; we're dancing. Suddenly, out of nowhere, he whispers to me to meet him outside, near some gazebo, back of the building, in half an hour. (*Short pause.*) Well, it was dark and drizzling standing out there by the old gazebo and more than half an hour had gone by, but I know I have to wait for him. So, I'm STANDING THERE getting really pissed off because I DON'T SEE ZORRO. Then, FINALLY I SEE HIM. But HE'S NOT WALKING TOWARD ME. Maybe I got his instructions wrong. So, I RUN UP TO HIM. And I throw my arms around him. THIS WAS MY BIG PLAY, SEE? So I'm kissing him. And suddenly he PICKS ME UP and carries me into these DARK BUSHES. I never would have expected anything SO DIRECT from Harrison. But there we were in the bushes. And there I was flat on my back with my Lizzie Borden skirt HIKED UP AND READY. (*Short pause.*) To make a long story short, it was the best sex I've ever had. (*Short pause.*) Only it wasn't Harrison. (*Slight pause.*) I guess Zorro was IN that year. (*Short pause.*) No. This rogue's name was Phillip Reynolds. A lower-middle-class medical student with a slightly more-than-genius I.Q. And the most jealous man I have ever met. (*Pause.*) I knew that night, there in the bushes with his sweat and his beautiful manhood; I knew that he had fallen madly in love with me. (*Short pause.*) But I also knew, that night, IN THAT MOMENT, that I would marry Harrison Brent. And leave Phillip Reynolds forever, (*Pause.*) It was after the Costume Ball I found out I was pregnant. But I wasn't sure who the father was. Harrison or Phillip. So, I gave it up. And I was ready to become MRS. BRENT. Ascher, I would have done anything to feel safe again. Now I do. (*SHE moves to kiss him.*)

ASCHER. I know you killed them

(*Slight pause. The PHONE rings.*)

MARGARET. (*Answering the phone.*) Yes.
(*Pause.*) No, of course I'm alone. (*Pause.*) I called
the airlines. You're booked on a ten a.m. out of
Kennedy. (*Pause.*) That's fine. See you soon.
(*Hangs up.*) He's coming back from the guest
house. You gotta get out of here!
ASCHER. He's gonna hear my car backing
out.
MARGARET. Put your car in neutral – roll it
down the driveway.
ASCHER. Is he going away?
MARGARET. I can't talk now! I'll call you
tomorrow!
ASCHER. Margaret.
MARGARET. GET OUT OR I'LL KILL YOU!

(*ASCHER exits. SHE arranges the room quickly.
Starts to go up the stairs. Ascher has left his tie
clip on the coffee table. HARRISON runs on
from the kitchen. Out of breath.*)

HARRISON. Who was here?
MARGARET. Lionel. He broke in at my
office.
HARRISON. (*Pause.*) He's almost ready
then.

MARGARET. Yes, he is. I'm seeing him again tomorrow after you leave.

HARRISON. You said he saw me at Mrs. Johaneston's on Monday night. He could describe me to the police!

MARGARET. I told you; he would never do that.

HARRISON. Are you sure you can handle this alone? I COULD stay till Sunday ...

MARGARET. No, you can't STAY TILL SUNDAY! They can't find you here. You have to leave TOMORROW!

HARRISON. Where's the baseball bat?

MARGARET. (*Short pause.*) In my office.

HARRISON. Your book's going to be a big hit.

MARGARET. Yes.

HARRISON. You're going to be a great success. (*Short pause.*) Come here. (*SHE does.*) It's what you always wanted, isn't it, Margaret? More than the money.

MARGARET. Yes, it is.

HARRISON. I gave up my practice.

MARGARET. I didn't ask you to.

HARRISON. Six months you said. I was doing very well.

MARGARET. I know.

HARRISON. Their problems were meaningless to me, though, you know? We never counted on THAT in college, did we? Do you remember the Costume Ball, Margaret?

MARGARET. Yes.

HARRISON. (*Grabbing her.*) I WANT TO POSSESS YOU AGAIN, CAN'T YOU UNDERSTAND THAT? DO YOU KNOW WHAT I'VE DONE FOR YOU? (*Slight pause.*) What about Ascher? DON'T LIE TO ME!

MARGARET. I'm going to have Lionel kill him on Sunday night.

HARRISON. I love you.

MARGARET. I love you.

HARRISON. Don't betray me.

MARGARET. I won't.

HARRISON. Don't ever leave me.

MARGARET. I w ...

HARRISON. TELL ME!

MARGARET. I LOVE YOU! I SWEAR IT! JUST YOU!

(*He kisses her savagely. Then abruptly, HE disengages and pulls away from her. Pause.*)

MARGARET. Why did you carve the A in Mrs. Johaneston's forehead?

HARRISON. (*Pause.*) Uh ... since there' s no link between you and ... Carlotta ... I thought it would remove you from suspicion.

MARGARET. (*Short pause.*) I'm tired. I'm going to sleep now. Oh, you'd better leave early tomorrow morning. It's a two hour drive to Kennedy. Have fun in London. Good night. (*SHE exits.*)

HARRISON. (*HE looks around. Finds Ascher's tie clip. Pause.*) "For James With Love." Ascher. (*Goes to phone. Dials.*) Yes, hello. I'm booked on your ten a.m. out of Kennedy for Heathrow, England. Could you help me? I want to change my reservation. I want to leave on Sunday night instead. (*Short pause.*) No, the midnight flight is fine. (*Short pause.*) My name? Reynolds. Phillip Reynolds. (*Short pause.*) Yah. I'll hold on.

FADE TO BLACK

Scene 6

Saturday afternoon. Two-twenty. In the darkness, we can hear someone moving a "tuning knob" along an AM radio dial. It's a jumble of SOUND, until:

FIRST ANNOUNCER. ... with this, the Commissioner vowed on the steps of the Chamber of Commerce to have a definite arrest of the Baseball Bat Killer within twenty-fours hours. He said he will, quote, "Look under every rock ..."

(*The TUNING continues. It will stop at the following station as the LIGHTS start up.*)

SECOND ANNOUNCER. Hello, ladies. And what a gorgeous Saturday afternoon it is. Now, put on those comfy shoes, because it's CHA-CHA TIME ALL OVER THE WORLD.

(*Loud cha-cha MUSIC. It's the next afternoon. Overcast. Gray LIGHT. The cha cha MUSIC will continue. LIONEL and MARGARET are standing center. Lionel's back is to us. HE is wearing a red dress, high heels, and a red wig. HE is trying to teach Margaret to cha-cha.*)

LIONEL. No. No. One-two, one-two-three. One-two, one- You're not trying! (*HE shuts MUSIC off.*) You still despise me, don't you? (*Short pause. HE produces a photograph.*) Here. (*HE gives it to Margaret.*) I took that picture this morning. My wife and daughter. Getting on a train. At Grand Central. They're both safe. They're going to Illinois. Her parents. I wasn't going to kill my daughter, if that's what you were thinking .Give me that picture back. Please.

(*SHE does.*)

LIONEL. (*Looks at the picture. Sits.*) I'll never forget her. She gave me much happiness. (*Short pause.*) She never blamed me. Her mother did. (*Short pause.*) I've done terrible things. Her lovers. Those men. (*Short pause.*) Terrible things. She forgave me. Her mother never knew. (*Short pause.*) You knew. That's why you chose me. Isn't that why you chose me? (*Short pause.*) Why you broke me down. Why you told me about Carlotta Donovan. (*Short pause.*) You killed that old woman, didn't you? The one I read about. The one who lived on Elm Street. You and that man killed her. You and that man killed Carlotta Donovan, too. (*Short pause.*) HE'S the baseball bat killer! Does he know I saw him on Elm Street on Monday night? You didn't tell him, did you?

MARGARET. He left for London this morning. Don't worry.

LIONEL. I never used a baseball bat. I made mine look like accidents. (*Short pause.*) When are the police coming?

MARGARET. Tomorrow night. Sunday night.

LIONEL. (*Rips the photo, slowly.*) Where's my gun?

MARGARET. Right here. (*SHE hands him the .45*)

LIONEL. I'll be ready for the police. (*Short pause.*) Does your husband know I'm staying the weekend?

MARGARET. (*Slight pause.*) My husband has been dead for six months.

LIONEL. (*Slight pause.*) Oh. (*Slight pause.*) So, I'll come down to your office.

MARGARET. Tomorrow night. When hear the clock chime.

LIONEL. TEN chimes. You promised I could hear that tape. Have it playing.

MARGARET. I will. Then go to sleep in my office.

LIONEL. Until I hear the timer.

MARGARET. (*Moves to desk and gets timer.*) *SHE rings it to demonstrate.*) Like this.

LIONEL. Then I come out.

MARGARET. Yes.

LIONEL. While you call the Commissioner.

MARGARET. Yes.

LIONEL. You want them to think I'M the baseball bat killer.

MARGARET. They will.

LIONEL. Good (*Pause.*) I think I told you my daughter made this dress. I want to be buried in it.

MARGARET. I have another dress for you to wear tomorrow night.

LIONEL. All right. (*Pause.*) I drove them in this morning. To the train station. We all sat in the front. (*Short pause.*) I kept thinking how they'd be reading the newspapers or watching T.V. next week in Illinois and seeing my face and some reporter calling me "the baseball bat killer." My wife will be livid. Because she's always been the successful one in my family. She'll be so jealous. She'll know how I felt in Paris when I pushed Richardson down that elevator shaft or when I blew that other guy's car up. (*Short pause.*) And while I was driving, I started thinking about the witch doctor in that painting. I was looking in the

rear view mirror at the traffic behind me and I
saw my eyes in the mirror and I started to panic. I
WASN'T THAT GUY IN THE MIRROR! I
WANTED TO PULL OVER, STOP THE CAR,
GET OUT MY TIRE IRON AND BEAT THEIR
BRAINS IN! I DIDN'T COME THIS FAR TO
HAVE THEM GET ON A TRAIN! – SO WHAT –
WHAT – THEY GET ON A TRAIN AND SIT BY
A WINDOW AND I'M ON THE PLATFORM
WAVING – WHO ARE THEY LOOKING AT?
THAT'S NOT ME! THIS ISN'T MY TALENT!
THIS IS WHAT HAPPENS TO A FAILURE! –
See, they wouldn't be waving goodbye to *me,* and I
wasn't going to let them get away with that. I
wanted them to remember me in the car, pulled
over, WIELDING A TIRE IRON! (*Pause.*) My
problem was that my daughter is the only creative
thing I've ever done. (*Short pause.*) So I felt
finally, if I could just get my daughter on that
train – (*Short pause.*) *I'd* be a success. (*Short
pause.*) And sure enough, there I was, standing on
the platform, waving, with the train pulling out
and both of them at a window waving back. And
the beauty of it was I didn't have to put on a
disguise this time to enjoy it. (*Slight pause.*) I was
already in disguise. (*Slight pause.*) But I had
forgotten to give my daughter my science medal.
You know, I told you about it. I was going to give it
to my daughter before she got on the train, because
I was thinking that I might not see her again for
years, maybe twenty years. How would she

recognize me? Then I thought of this science medal. Pretty smart, huh? Now, you're probably thinking that any thirty-five thousand people might have this kind of science medal. But look. There's an inscription. That's how you could tell. By reading the inscription.

MARGARET. (*Not looking at medal.*) "Manchester, W.H."

LIONEL. (*Short pause.*) MANCHESTER W.H.? NO! It doesn't say that at all. (*Short pause.*) So I was going to give it to her. (*Short pause.*) But the truth is I won't be around in twenty years. (*Short pause.*) So, I want you to have it. In case she comes back. (*Pause.*) I'm going upstairs now, okay? (*HE stands.*)

MARGARET. Okay.

LIONEL. I DO remind you of someone else. Don't I?

MARGARET. (*Short pause.*) My husband.

LIONEL. (*Short pause.*) And I WAS right about his painting.

MARGARET. Yes, you were.

LIONEL. (*Short pause.*) I have too much PRIDE to kill myself. I just couldn't do it. (*Pause.*) Good luck. (*Hands her the medal. Goes up the stairs. Exits.*)

MARGARET. (*SHE moves to the phone. Dials.*) Is Inspector Ascher by any chance working today? Would you connect me with him, please? Thank you. (*Short pause.*) Hi. It's me. How are you? I was thinking about you. Are you

busy tomorrow night? (*Short pause.*) Let's make
up. Let's go to Hartford. Have you ever been to
Angelina's? Because they have the BEST ...
(*Short pause.*) No. *Don't* wear that BROWN
JACKET. They won't let you in. My advice is to
charge it to the Commissioner, if you can. (*Short
pause.*) What? Oh, come on, Ascher, GET OFF
THE NIGHTMARE! I told you, we were ACTING
OUT her nightmare and I ... No, *I* was calling
him, from upstairs. Yes, we have four different
phone lines. Even one at the guest house. I'm
decadent, what can I say? Anyway, about
tomorrow night. Could you pick me up around
ten? Let's say ten-o-five. Or thereabouts. (*Short
pause.*) Great. I'll be ready for you at ten-o-five.
(*Short pause.*) Me too. I have to go now. Goodbye.
(*Margaret is about to hang up the phone.*) Hello?
Hello? Is there someone else on this line? Hello?

BLACKOUT

Scene 7

Sunday night. Ten o'clock. In the darkness we
hear a CLOCK chiming. Light comes into the
room, but it's dim. The office LIGHT is on,
though. There is a reel-to-reel tape recorder
sitting on the coffee table with some small box-

*like device hooked up to it and on the tenth
chime, this device goes off. It's a timer, which
causes the tape recorder to go on. We hear
MOZART again. And a THUNDERSTORM.
Someone in the office turns the LIGHT out.
LIONEL appears on the landing. HE's in a
green dress and the red wig. HE has a gun in
his hand. HE stands there a moment. The
MUSIC is "Dissonance" from the string
quartet in C major. LIONEL descends,
holding the gun up, as if to rehearse. HE halts
at the foot of the steps, pointing the gun at the
painting. A MAN leaps out of the office at
Lionel; HE has grabbed at Lionel's gun-hand
and is covering Lionel's mouth. HE drags
him into the office. We notice very quickly
that the man is PHILLIP REYNOLDS. A
THUNDERCLAP from the tape recorder. And
then, an awful THUD from the office: a
CRACKING SOUND. It could be the sound of a
bat breaking a cantaloupe. But it isn't. The
SOUND repeats as LIONEL screams again
from the office. The MUSIC is loud, the storm
consistent. PHILLIP REYNOLDS is grunting
from the office, even after Lionel is quiet. We
hear a BASEBALL BAT being dropped to the
floor. Suddenly we hear a DOOR open and
close. PHILLIP REYNOLDS emerges from
the office; HE has blood on him. Suddenly,
another MAN'S VOICE is heard on the tape*

recorder. We have never heard this man's voice before.

TAPE   LIVE ACTION.
RUNNING.

OTHER   *(PHILLIP*
MAN'S VOICE.   *REYNOLDS closes*
PUPPY! (*Slight*   *the office door,*
pause.*) Puppy,   *moves to the*
where are you?   *landing, looking*
MARGARET'S   *up, making sure no*
VOICE.   *one has heard. HE*
I'm in the kitchen!   *stands there a*
                        moment.
(The MUSIC stops;   *HE reaches into his*
the storm   *pocket for a*
continues.)   *handkerchief, and*
                        wipes himself as
OTHER MAN'S   *HE moves toward*
VOICE.   *the kitchen. HE has*
You know I hate   *gone into the*
this music. Why do   *kitchen.)*
you play it?
MARGARET'S
VOICE.
You were outside.

OTHER MAN'S
VOICE. (*Slight
pause.*) Your tape
recorder is
running.

MARGARET'S
VOICE.
Yes, Harrison – I
was working.
(*So this is the voice
of the real Harrison
Brent.*)

HARRISON
BRENT'S VOICE.
You'll be late for the
British Club. Is that
what you're
wearing?

MARGARET'S
VOICE.
Don't you like it?

HARRISON
BRENT'S VOICE.
Why are they
giving you a
trophy?

MARGARET'S
VOICE.
My series of
articles in the
Times.

HARRISON   *(PHILLIP*
BRENT'S VOICE.   *REYNOLDS*
Yes. I read them.   *emerges from the*
They were   *kitchen carrying a*
childish.   *suitcase and a coat.*
                           HE checks the
MARGARET'S   *landing again. No*
VOICE.   *one there. HE puts*
Really?   *the suitcase down.*

HARRISON   *HE fishes in a coat*
BRENT'S VOICE.   *pocket.*
You're trying to
make psychiatry
flashy. I was
writing about
psychodrama ten
years ago.
                           HE has produced an
MARGARET'S   *airline ticket. HE*
VOICE.   *inspects it.*
Yes, but you
stopped.

HARRISON
BRENT'S VOICE.
I RETIRED. Must
you mock my
sickness as though
I were making
excuses?

*HE puts the ticket
back into the coat
pocket.*

MARGARET'S
VOICE.
I wasn't mocking
your ...

HARRISON
BRENT'S VOICE.
I found that
manuscript in your
desk. (*Short pause.*)
Have you gotten a
publisher? (*Slight
pause.*)

MARGARET'S
VOICE.
Not yet.

*HE picks up the
suitcase. HE stands
there, listening.*

HARRISON
BRENT'S VOICE.
You're going to
have everything
you always wanted,
Margaret. I'm so
happy for you.
MARGARET'S
VOICE.
I saw you talking to
Carlotta Donovan
on the footpath.
(*Slight pause.*)

HARRISON
BRENT'S VOICE.
YES. She was
telling me how
fascinating my
PAINTING IS.

MARGARET'S
VOICE.
I've told you NOT to
bother my patients!
HARRISON
BRENT'S VOICE.
She's been having
this TERRIBLE
nightmare —

MARGARET'S
VOICE.
I know that —
HARRISON
BRENT'S VOICE.
YOU HAVEN'T
EVEN BEEN
LISTENING TO
HER; YOU'RE SO
HUNGRY TO
PUBLISH THAT
BOOK. She knows
you don't like her.

*HE heads for the
front door. HE goes
out quickly,
shutting the door
behind him.*

MARGARET'S
VOICE.
She's cold and she
lies.

HARRISON
BRENT'S VOICE.
But you're going to
be late for the
British Club.
(*Slight pause.*)

MARGARET'S
VOICE.
Why are you so
anxious for me to
go?

HARRISON BRENT'S VOICE. Oh, please, Margaret – you've ALWAYS been leaving me. You were just looking for the right opportunity, yes? I'm going upstairs. I want to find my cummerbund. (*We hear him going upstairs.*)

MARGARET'S VOICE. I'll be home early.

(*From upstairs, we hear Margaret's voice.*)

HARRISON BRENT'S VOICE. TAKE YOUR TIME. I'LL CALL YOU WHEN I'M READY. (*Short pause, and HE's gone.*)

MARGARET'S VOICE. (*From upstairs.*) THESE SHOES ARE KILLING ME!

MARGARET'S
VOICE.
WHAT DID YOU
SAY? HARRISON?
(*We hear papers
RUSTLING;
Margaret's voice is
coming closer.
Quieter.*) Jerk.
(*Short pause.*) Um.   (*MARGARET
I can't finish this   appears on the
now. Patient S-2.   landing, in
She's still harping   evening dress.
about that   SHE descends and
nightmare. I don't   heads directly for
know why she   the office door. SHE
dislikes me so   knocks on the
much. She said   door.*)
again today that she
didn't know why
the woman's voice
says "I hate you" in
the nightmare. I
have to analyze this
nightmare. I'm
suspicious. She's
hiding something
from me. Also,
she's jealous of our
money.

She keeps asking about my clothes, my jewelry. Maybe she's been coming on to Harrison. That's a laugh. Damn, I have to leave. Where's my bracelet? I'll finish this when I get back from the British Club. (*Slight pause. A CLICK. No sound. Then another CLICK, and the THUNDER-STORM again, and that GIRL'S VOICE from the opening scene. It is Carlotta Donovan's voice.*) CARLOTTA DONOVAN'S VOICE. Dr.Brent, Margaret, I'm using your tape recorder. I know you're at the British Club.

MARGARET. (*Knocking.*) Lionel. Are you sleeping? (*SHE opens the door a crack. The LIGHT is off.*) Lionel? (*Pause. SHE closes the door and moves to the stereo. SHE opens the cabinet under the stereo and pulls out another timer, sets it, wraps it in a sweater, puts it back and closes the cabinet. SHE sits in the armchair listening to the tape.*)

(The DOORBELL SOUNDS and MARGARET quickly shuts the tape off. The doorbell is the famous ten notes in "Non Piu Andrai" from The Marriage of Figaro. MARGARET hesitates, and mutters.)

MARGARET. He would find the doorbell tonight.

(SHE picks up recorder and moves to office door. SHE reaches door and realizes Lionel is asleep inside and can't wake him yet. SHE puts recorder on desk chair. DOORBELL rings again. SHE moves to front door. Turns on overhead LIGHT and opens door.)

ASCHER. *(Standing in the doorway. HE has on a coat.)* Under the "Beware of Dog" sign. Very clever.

MARGARET. Just come in. Excuse me for a second. *(SHE crosses into kitchen.)*

(HE does. Closes door. HE starts to speak. The STEREO LIGHT goes on. MOZART again, the String Quartet in C Major.)

ASCHER. How did you do that?

(Short pause.)

MARGARET. (*In kitchen.*) You were one minute early. What can I say? I put a timer inside that liquor cabinet thing. (*SHE enters.*) I thought we'd appetize HERE before facing Angelina. (*SHE puts a dish of McNuggets on the coffee table.*) There's McNuggets on the coffee table.

ASCHER. (*Has opened the cabinet. Looking.*) Why the sweater?

MARGARET. (*As SHE moves to kitchen.*) I can't hear you!

(*ASCHER takes his coat off. HE's in a tuxedo. Moves toward office door. MARGARET comes out of kitchen. Real quick.*)

MARGARET. Oh, let me take that STUPID COAT. (*Takes coat.*) Why don't you have a McNugget while I get the champagne?

ASCHER. You gonna tell me about the sweater?

MARGARET. (*Has gone back into kitchen with Ascher's coat. In kitchen.*) I use a timer for my session. For my patients.

ASCHER. How? For what reason?

MARGARET. (*In kitchen.*) To let me know when the session is over. Music goes off.

ASCHER. Why don't you use a clock? Don't you wear a watch?

MARGARET. (*Entering.*) HEY! MY SESSIONS END OR BEGIN AT TEN AFTER THE HOUR, and no, I don't wear a watch.

ASCHER. So?

MARGARET. Look. (*SHE crosses to stereo.*) I put the tape in the cassette player. (*Turns off tape deck.*) Then, I set the little timer. (*SHE does.*) Then, I put the timer in the cabinet. (*SHE does.*) Now HERE'S THE HARD PART, Inspector. SINCE I DON'T WANT TO MAKE THEM QUADRUPLY NERVOUS WITH ALL THAT EEEEEHHHHH, I PUT MOTHER'S UGLY SWEATER OVER IT. AND, HOPING YOU LIKE MOZART AS MUCH AS I DO, I CLOSE MR. CABINET. AND YOU'D NEVER KNOW ANYTHING WAS AMISS, EH? (*SHE walks back into the kitchen.*)

ASCHER. Yup. (*Pause.*)

(*MARGARET stands in the kitchen doorway. SHE is holding, in each hand, a champagne glass, filled. Pause.*)

MARGARET. I hope your wife won't be expecting you tonight. (*Slight pause.*) My husband left for Europe yesterday morning. He's gone. (*Slight pause.*) What I'm saying is if you want to stay here with me. (*Slight pause.*) Could be fun. No? (*Slight pause.*) I think we hit if off. Don't you? You're a good *guy*. (*Slight pause.*) I'd be perfectly willing to share the wealth, if you know what I mean. (*Pause.*) I love you. (*Slight pause.*) Here. Let's have REAL champagne. (*Gives glass.*) To ...? To what. To tonight. My book is a smash and I go on Donahue tomorrow. (*Slight pause.*) To Margaret Thorne. Just Margaret Thorne. C'mon.

(*Slowly, ASCHER hands the glass back to Margaret. Pause.*)

ASCHER. It's too late for that, Margaret.

(*Slight pause.*)

MARGARET. What are you talking about?

ASCHER. (*Slight pause.*) I'm talking about last Sunday night. When you and Phillip were acting out the nightmare. You used timers?

MARGARET. (*Slight pause.*) Is that against the law?

ASCHER. Why?

MARGARET. Because we only have four hands.

ASCHER. You need to have EVERYTHING EXACT.

MARGARET. If I'm ever to solve the nightmare, RIGHT!

ASCHER. The nightmare: a clock chiming ten, rock music, the guy yelling on the phone "How are your British Club friends? What a SPEECH you must've made," and the girl's voice from your office: everything Mrs. Johaneston witnessed last Sunday night you're saying was the girl's nightmare?

MARGARET. RIGHT!

ASCHER. There's no phone call from the British Club in the girl's nightmare.

MARGARET. (*Pause.*) What does that tell you?

ASCHER. Last Sunday night, you and Phillip Reynolds were re-enacting your husband's murder. (*Slight pause.*)

MARGARET. That's ridiculous.

ASCHER. Six months ago the British Club of Hartford, Connecticut presented you this TROPHY at a banquet.

MARGARET. Like I said.

ASCHER. At that banquet you made a SPEECH.

MARGARET. They loved me.

ASCHER. Then there was an emergency. You had to go to a phone and call your husband.

MARGARET. YES! –

ASCHER. I THINK YOUR HUSBAND WAS HERE WITH YOUR PATIENT. I think *they* were "acting out" her nightmare and YOU CALLED FROM THE BRITISH CLUB. Your husband answered the phone, and you had a big argument. (*Slight pause.*) This is what you were re-enacting last Sunday night.

MARGARET. PROVE IT!

ASCHER. I CAN'T. (*Pause.*)

MARGARET. (*Moving towards him.*) I said I'd share the money.

ASCHER. (*Slight pause.*) I had Scotty's Pond dragged again at five o'clock this morning.

MARGARET. (*Pause.*) Did you.
ASCHER. Where's my coat? (*Short pause.*)
MARGARET. In the kitchen.

(*ASCHER moves to the kitchen. MARGARET moves swiftly to her desk to get timer. As SHE is about to open her office door to awaken Lionel with timer, she hears ASCHER yell from kitchen: "Found it." MARGARET puts timer back on desk. As Ascher enters with his coat, HE is rummaging through the pockets for something. HE has his gun, a .38 special in one hand, while HE digs through the coat pocket with his other hand.*)

ASCHER. Giarrusso got these guys from Boston to drag the pond for two hundred bucks. The Commissioner would have had my ass. (*Has a brown package in his hand. The package is a small bag. HE throws coat over arm of couch and puts his gun on the coffee table.*) I thought there might be something ELSE in the pond. Something we might've missed six months ago when we found the dead girl.
MARGARET. Lemme guess. Whatever you found is in that little bag.
ASCHER. That's right.
MARGARET. Am I going to have a heart attack when you show me?
ASCHER. No. I think you want to get caught.

MARGARET. WILL YOU JUST SHOW ME WHAT'S IN THE BAG!

ASCHER. (*Produces a square silverish object.*) See. Somebody tried to BURN it. Then threw it in the pond. Lady's makeup kit. Initials. C.D. (*Pause.*)

(*During this speech, MARGARET takes the timer off her desk and moves to the office to awake Lionel. SHE opens office door, turns on office LIGHT, looks inside, and suddenly closes the door quickly. SHE has seen Lionel dead. SHE puts the timer back on her desk and stands, leaning on her desk.*)

ASCHER. So you came back from the British Club. You saw that this girl had killed your husband. You killed her, and threw the body in the pond. I still don't know what you did with your husband's body.

MARGARET. (*Pause.*) Why would this girl kill my husband?

ASCHER. (*Slight pause.*) Why'd she kill him? I don't know why. (*HE looks at painting.*) I think THIS is why. (*HE moves to fireplace. His back is to Margaret.*)

MARGARET. You'd make a lousy psychiatrist.

ASCHER. Listen. If I can figure this painting out, I'll have what I want.

MARGARET. Want some help? (*MARGARET takes Ascher's gun from the coffee table. SHE will hide it behind her back, for now.*)

ASCHER. The puppy is YOU.

MARGARET. Right.

ASCHER. The guy with the holes in his arm is your husband.

MARGARET. Always.

ASCHER. Now this person with the flamboyant pose. This is supposed to be some kind of WITCH DOCTOR?

MARGARET. Could be.

ASCHER. And the skull I could figure out. Tell me, Doctor, what's YOUR interpretation of this painting?

MARGARET. (*Short pause.*) Okay. The man on his knees is crawling away from DEATH: the skull. He meets some voodoo person and asks HOW can he reach the puppy.

ASCHER. He can SEE the puppy.

MARGARET. Maybe he needs MEDICAL HELP in order to reach the puppy. Or, better yet, maybe HE'S ASKING ME TO HELP HIM FIND THE WOMAN HE THOUGHT I WAS.

ASCHER. (*Pause.*) Why didn't you? Help him. (*HE is now looking at Margaret.*)

MARGARET. (*Short pause.*) For starters, I'm not a puppy.

ASCHER. Where's my gun?

MARGARET. (*Points gun at him.*) Don't move. (*Pause.*) See – I told you it was possible to get a gun away from a cop. (*Pause.*) You still haven't shown me what's in the makeup kit.

ASCHER. (*Slight pause.*) I'd assumed you already knew that.

MARGARET. No. I just tried to burn it. Besides, the damn thing wouldn't open! I kept throwing it on the ground. I even drove my car over it. I just wanted to see what was in it. Now I can. You DID manage to get it open, didn't you?

ASCHER. There's a CATCH. It pops open. (*HE does it.*)

MARGARET. Stupid thing.

ASCHER. Giarrusso examined this stuff. He didn't find anything.

MARGARET. But you did.

ASCHER. Yeah, sure.

MARGARET. I knew you were trouble the first day I met you.

ASCHER. I hated your guts the first day I met you.

MARGARET. But you feel differently now.

ASCHER. Yes, I do. (*Short pause.*) I love you.

MARGARET. (*Slight pause.*) You're just saying that because I'm holding a gun on you.

ASCHER. (*Slight pause.*) Would I have put my gun on your coffee table if I thought you could shoot me ?

MARGARET. I HAVE TO SHOOT YOU. First, you caught me in those lies about where my husband was. (*Dialing the phone.*) Then, you figured out the signatures. Now, I ...

ASCHER. I DIDN'T FIGURE OUT THE SIGNATURES.

MARGARET. BUT YOU KNEW SOMETHING WAS WRONG. YOU WERE CLOSE. (*ASCHER starts to speak.*) SHUTTUP! I'LL KILL YOU! (*Into phone.*) Hello, could I speak to the Commissioner, please? This is an emergency.

ASCHER. WHAT ARE YOU CALLING THE COMMISSIONER FOR?

MARGARET. NO! (*Into phone.*) No, I can talk to you. This is Doctor Margaret Thorne Brent. I have just killed one of my patients. He broke in the house with a baseball bat; he said he was that killer. He struggled with Inspector Ascher; the gun went off. I grabbed the baseball bat. Please come quickly to Lakehill Road. Help me! (*Hangs up quickly.*)

ASCHER. MARGARET LISTEN TO ME – THERE'S A WAY OUT OF THIS.

MARGARET. I CAN'T STOP NOW. (*SHE takes the phone receiver off the hook and slams it on the desk.*) I hate you for making me do this. I offered you millions; what're you, crazy? ... (*Short pause.*) What is that in your hand?

ASCHER. (*Looks in his hand.*) Uh ... she kept things in a secret compartment. (*Holds up a tiny crucifix.*) I found this crucifix in it.

MARGARET. (*Pause.*) Is that the end of it?

ASCHER. (*Slight pause.*) There's something WRITTEN across the back ...

MARGARET. Yes.
ASCHER. You want me to read it?
MARGARET. Yes.
ASCHER. (*Reading.*) "Manchester W.H."
That's it.

(*Pause. MARGARET drops the gun. A beeping
[off the hook] sound emerges from the phone.*)

ASCHER. Margaret? What is it?
MARGARET. (*Pause.*) The police will be here
any minute. (*SHE moves the lamp next to the
armchair. The BEEPING has stopped.*) Harrison
had broken the outside light. There was rock
music still playing. (*SHE turns the overhead
LIGHT down; the room is dim.*) I started to go
upstairs. (*Short pause.*) My office door was closed,
but the light was on. (*SHE opens office door.*)
Harrison was lying on the sofa. Dressed in a
tuxedo. He had been shot many times. He was
dead. She was lying face down on the floor. Near
the window. Wearing a green dress. My medical
bag was open and my tape recorder was running.
(*Short pause.*) I could've prevented this. (*Short
pause.*) They had acted out her nightmare, only
Harrison put REAL bullets in her gun. (*Slight
pause.*) She must've tried to save him. She had
taken my scalpel and carved the letter A in her
forehead. She must've slept with him. She had
swallowed a whole bottle of pills. She left me a
message on my tape recorder and then she died.

(*Pause.*) I couldn't report it. She would be a murderess and I would be a pauper. (*Short pause.*) I burned her clothes. I took a baseball bat and disfigured her so she couldn't be recognized. I threw her in Scotty's Pond. And then I made a long distance call. To Phillip Reynolds. In London. I told him I loved him, that I had always loved him. He agreed to impersonate Harrison. (*Slight pause.*) And every Sunday night, I've been RE-ENACTING what happened, because she said she left me one clue and I didn't know what it was until now.

ASCHER. (*Slight pause.*) Why did you have Phillip KILL Mrs. Johaneston?

MARGARET. Last Sunday night. When she saw us. And then Monday when you read me her statement. I told Phillip. He said she had to go.

ASCHER. Why?

MARGARET. While we were acting out the nightmare. She saw him eat a piece of cake. (*Pause.*) She would've told everybody.

ASCHER. (*Pause.*) What about this? (*HE holds up the crucifix.*)

MARGARET. Can I have that, please? (*HE gives it to her.*) She had black hair when she was born. (*Pause.*) I was in England when I found out I was pregnant. I checked into a hospital. In Manchester. There was a nun assigned to me. Sister Marie. They had nuns there to talk you into giving up your baby. But Sister Marie held my hand. She was wise to me. She knew I didn't want it. (*Slight pause.*) I remember running down this corridor as they were taking it away because Sister Marie had given me a crucifix that I wanted my little girl to have. In case I ever saw her again. (*Slight pause.*) That was eighteen years ago. At the Manchester Women's Hospital. And this is it. (*Pause.*) This is it. (*Slight pause.*) This is it.

ASCHER. (*Pause. Suddenly looking at painting.*) Harrison killed himself. So, the guy SHOULD be crawling towards the skull. (*Short pause.*) He switched the bricks. (*Short pause.*) Why? (*Pause.*) YOU switched the bricks. (*Pause.*) YOU BURIED HIM IN THE FIREPLACE! (*Pause.*) You took out the bricks. Put in the body. You put it BACK like this.

MARGARET. (*Very slight pause.*) That's just how I did it.

ASCHER. (*Very slight pause.*) I still don't know who the witch doctor is.

MARGARET. (*Short pause.*) Inspector?

ASCHER. Yes, Margaret?

MARGARET. I think you should go look in my office now.

(*Short pause. ASCHER goes into office. We can hear SIRENS. MARGARET picks up Ascher's gun. SHE puts the nozzle to her temple. Her hands are shaking. SHE closes her eyes. SHE pulls the trigger. The GUN goes off. SHE falls to the floor. ASCHER runs out of office. Loud*

SIRENS. ASCHER kneels beside Margaret. HE's checking the wound.)

ASCHER. Margaret. I put blanks in the gun. (*Pause.*) You've got a burn here. It didn't pierce your skin. Margaret?

(*SHE opens her eyes. ASCHER has a handkerchief next to the wound. MARGARET looks up at him. Pause. She's crying.*)

MARGARET. Ascher. (*Pause.*) She must've thought I'd never forgive her. (*Pause.*) Because she never forgave me.
ASCHER. (*Short pause.*) That's why she killed herself.
MARGARET. (*Short pause.*) Ascher?
ASCHER. Yes, Margaret.
MARGARET. You're kneeling on my hair.
ASCHER. Sorry.

(*HE helps her to the chair. SIRENS coming up the driveway. ASCHER throws open the front door. SIRENS. Red and blue FLASHING LIGHTS. The STEREO LIGHT goes on. That MOZART piece. ASCHER moves to the stereo.*)

MARGARET. Let it play.

(*HE moves to the office entrance. Looks at Margaret. Comes back to her. Touches her arm.*)

MARGARET. I'll be all right.
ASCHER. I still love you.

(*Pause. HE goes into the office. MARGARET alone. SIRENS. MUSIC. SHE stares out. Thinking.*)

SLOWEST FADE TO BLACK

THE PLAY IS OVER

© COPYRIGHT 1987

PERFECT CRIME
FIREPLACE PAINTING

KILLING THE KING

by Margaret Thorne Brent

Margaret Thorne Brent / KILLING THE KING

Actor Photograph

COSTUME PLOT

ACT I

Scene 1

MAN: black tuxedo, white shirt, **red cummerbund** and bow tie, black gloves
GIRL: green dress, red wig

Scene 2

MARGARET: pants and blouse, smock, goggles
ASCHER: suit
HARRISON: pants, sleeveless tee-shirt, then shirt

Scene 3

LIONEL: sports jacket, pants, shirt and tie
MARGARET: pants, blouse and jacket

Scene 4

HARRISON: smoking jacket, turtleneck and tuxedo pants
ASCHER: brown jacket and pants, shirt, tie
MARGARET: running outfit

ACT II

<u>Scene 5</u>

LIONEL: jeans, shirt, dark jacket
MARGARET: skirt and blouse (at home evening wear)
ASCHER: jacket and pants, shirt, tie
HARRISON: blazer, turtleneck, pants

<u>Scene 6</u>

LIONEL: red dress, red wig, high-heeled shoes
MARGARET: sweater and pants

<u>Scene 7</u>

LIONEL: green dress, red wig, high heeled shoes
PHILLIP: sports jacket, shirt and pants, raincoat
MARGARET: black evening dress
ASCHER: raincoat, black tuxedo, black cummerbund and bow tie

PROPERTY PLOT

ACT I

Scene 1

On Stage:

Gun (.45) on desk
Tray of pastry on coffee table
Magazines on coffee table (for entire play)
Trophy on bookshelf (for entire play)

Personal:

A watch and gloves (MAN)
Gun (GIRL)

Scene 2

On Stage:

Checkbook, pen, and American Express folder on
    desk

Personal:

Electric drill, bit and goggles (MARGARET)
Notebook, Miranda rights, and a police artist's
    rendering of W. Harrison Brent as described
    by Mrs. Johaneston (ASCHER)

Scene 3

On Stage:

Different tray of pastry on coffee table

Off Stage:

Box of corn flakes (LIONEL)
A gun and a wig box with red wig in it (LIONEL)

Personal:

A watch, and a cassette recorder with cassette; a
    sealed envelope addressed to the *New York
    Times* (LIONEL)

Scene 4

On Stage:

Different tray of pastry on coffee table

Off Stage:

Two champagne glasses with champagne
    (HARRISON)
Three folding chairs (MARGARET)

Personal:

Rifle with cleaning rag (HARRISON)
Badge, receipt, wedding ring, pen, cigarette
    lighter, and a tie clip backwards on tie
    (ASCHER)

ACT II

Scene 5

On Stage:

Different tray of pastry on coffee table
Bottle of Johnny Walker Black and two glasses
Work folder on desk

Off Stage:

Ice (MARGARET)

Personal:

Notebook and pen, tie clip on tie, and a copy of
    Margaret's book *Killing the King* (ASCHER)

Scene 6

On Stage:

.45 automatic on mantle
Timer on desk

Personal:

A photograph and a science medal (LIONEL)

Scene 7

On Stage:

Different tray of pastry on coffee table
Reel-to-reel tape recorder with timer attached to it
    on coffee table
Another timer and a sweater inside cabinet near
    stereo

Off Stage:

Chicken McNuggets and two champagne glasses
    with champagne (MARGARET)
Baseball bat, suitcase, and airline ticket
    (PHILLIP)

Personal:

Gun (LIONEL)
Handkerchief (PHILLIP)
Paper bag containing a make-up kit with a
    crucifix inside, a gun and a handkerchief
    (ASCHER)

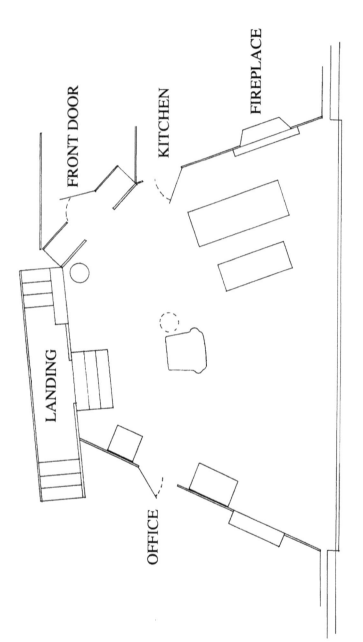

FRONT DOOR

KITCHEN

FIREPLACE

LANDING

OFFICE

PERFECT CRIME

.

Milton Keynes UK
Ingram Content Group UK Ltd.
UKHW020207150924
448317UK00010B/102

9 780573 691522